Free to Kill

CATCH, RELEASE, REPEAT

WILLIAM M. STANTON

PAGE PUBLISHING
Conneaut Lake, PA

First originally published by Page Publishing 2024

ISBN 979-8-89157-943-9 (pbk)
ISBN 979-8-89157-961-3 (digital)

Printed in the United States of America

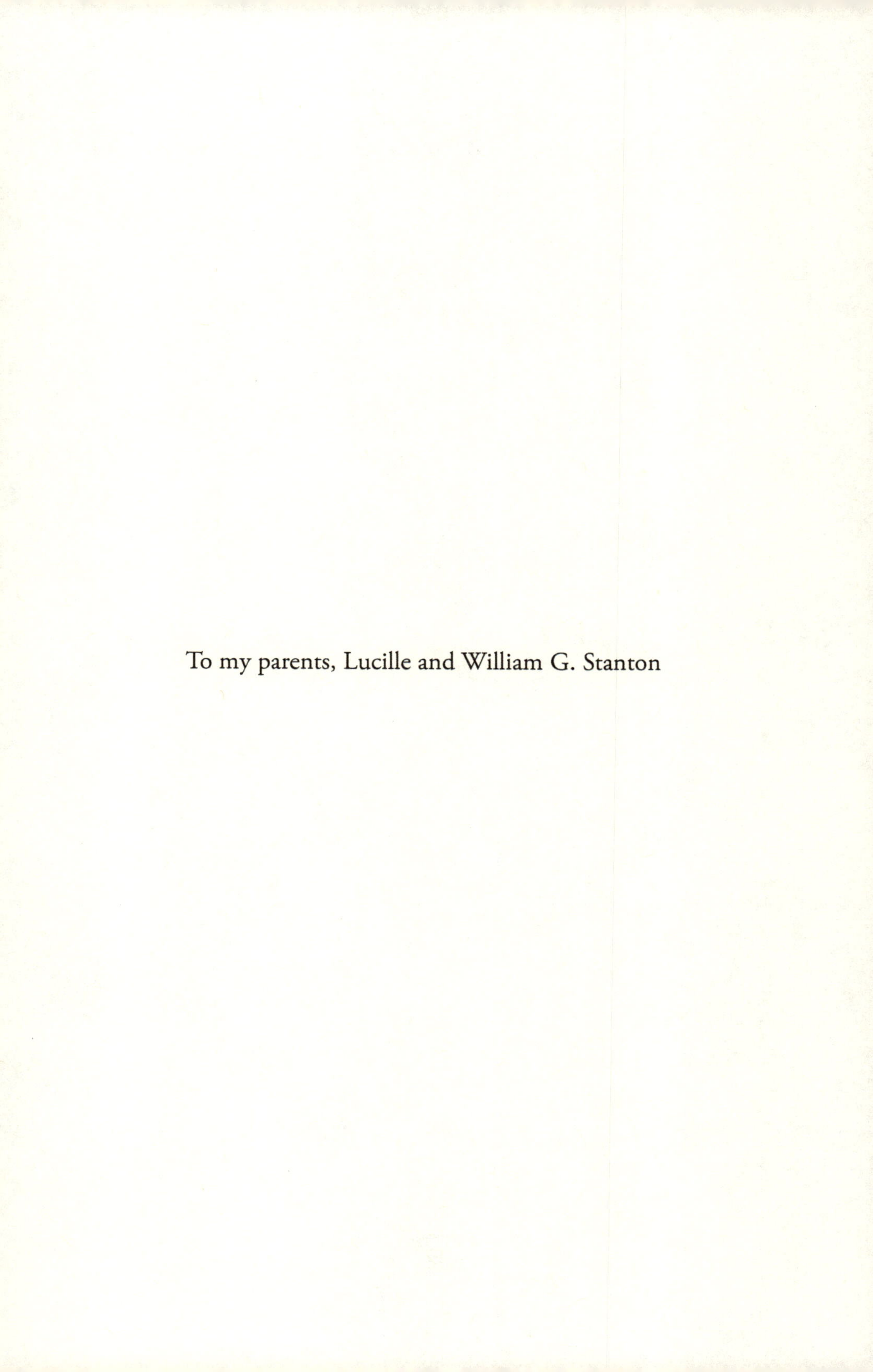
To my parents, Lucille and William G. Stanton

P R O L O G U E

April 1978
Hackensack River, Secaucus, New Jersey

The first thing that hit him was the smell. At first, he was grateful to get out of the back seat of the detectives' unmarked car and breathe some fresh air. The seat had a stale odor—the essence of old vomit, urine, and perspiration. The sweat pouring off the overweight, pissed-off detective didn't help.

They were ordered by the chief of detectives, Captain O'Brien, to go to a deserted area of Secaucus, New Jersey, on the banks of the highly polluted Hackensack River. The objective of this trip was to search for two missing children from West Hoboken. The children left for school almost two weeks ago and never returned home.

The detectives initially theorized that the father, whom they regarded as some kind of religious fanatic, had murdered the girl to cover up an incestuous relationship, with the boy being collateral damage.

Bill Stanford didn't believe that for a minute. He was not a cop, but he worked part-time for Police Commissioner Johnson.

Johnson was a friend of his, and Stanford had worked hard to get him elected. In the tradition of Hudson County machine politics, he was rewarded with a patronage job at city hall to supplement his meager teaching salary, his actual profession.

One of Stanford's duties was to act as a press spokesman, which brought him into contact with a woman named Betty Collins. She had read a newspaper article mentioning his name and called him at city hall.

"Hello, Police Commissioner's Office, Stanford speaking," he answered.

"Hi, Mr. Stanford. My name is Betty Collins, and I know where those two children are."

After the shock wore off, he questioned her thoroughly. He learned that she was a psychic who had a vision of the two children lying dead near a body of water in an isolated area. She claimed they were near a railroad bridge and an abandoned factory. She lived in Rutherford and had worked with the River Valley police force in the past.

"You probably think I'm a nut, but contact Lt. Stew Jacobs as a reference. He can vouch for me," she said. "Please hurry. I can't bear to think of those two little angels lying there, disposed of like pieces of garbage," she begged.

Stanford didn't know if she was nuts or genuine. She certainly sounded sincere. He decided to call Lt. Jacobs at the River Valley police. He confirmed that she had indeed helped them in a missing persons case, although he was, like Stanford, very dubious at first.

Stanford decided to take this information to his superiors, setting up a meeting with Mayor Vincent Corso, Police Commissioner Johnson, and Captain Wilber O'Brien.

All were highly skeptical initially, especially old-school Captain O'Brien. Stanford pointed out to him that for the past two weeks, his police force was being hammered by the press for being "shockingly inept" in their efforts to find these kids who, after this length of time, were almost certainly dead. This wasn't a kidnapping. There were no ransom demands, and the family didn't have a pot to piss in.

"Why not give her a try?" he implored the group.

Mayor Corso, who was also a powerful state senator, led the charge to bring the New York Giants to the New Jersey Meadowlands in a brand-new stadium, built alongside the also brand-new Meadowlands Racetrack. An NHL hockey franchise and NBA basketball team were being planned for a yet-to-be-built, state-of-the-art arena within the same complex.

All these accomplishments had Senator Corso on the shortlist of Democratic Party candidates for governor, but in his dual role as mayor of West Hoboken, this ugly child disappearance case was generating lots of bad press that he couldn't afford at this crucial time in his political career.

"Let Billy check this out," he roared in his raspy voice to Captain O'Brien. "Unofficial, like no press. This way, your crack police force won't be embarrassed that they're working with a fortune teller. Billy, take her out to lunch out of town. Find out what you can and get back to us," he commanded.

Stanford did as he was ordered, and this was how he wound up in a smelly police car in the swamps of Secaucus. He and the two detectives met a uniformed Secaucus policeman in a nearby parking lot as a courtesy, as it was their jurisdiction.

The four of them spread out and walked toward the riverbank through soft, muddy soil. Detective Shack complained loudly that we were ruining his new, expensive Italian shoes.

Betty had told Stanford at lunch, among other things, that there was a red burlap bag near the bodies. He was concentrating on this, reasoning that something red would stand out against the brownish-gray soil and high weeds.

The river smelt bad. It had been used as a dumping ground by chemical plants for years. Despite this, foolhardy souls still fished and crabbed there, ignoring signs not to eat anything that came out of it.

As they went further along the deserted bank, the smell became worse and somehow different. It reminded Stanford of the time he was little and a stray cat had died in their backyard.

He thought he saw the red burlap bag ahead to the right and quickened his pace. As he neared it, he realized it wasn't a red bag but a red polka-dot dress hanging off the dead body of little Esmeralda Gomez. Her hands were tied in front of her—as Betty had told him—and her panties were pulled down to her ankles.

Little Jesus's body was floating face down, halfway in and halfway out of the water, at the tide line twenty yards downstream.

Stanford was twenty-seven years old, and the only dead bodies he had seen were in funeral parlors, nicely arranged and perfumed with flowers. This was nothing like that. He fought the urge to vomit, not wanting to appear weak in front of those so-called "macho cops"—until Detective Shack, who he didn't realize had joined him, puked loudly into the weeds.

Officer Stevens of the Secaucus police stepped up and keyed his radio. "Call the county. This is a murder scene. We need the coroner and forensic teams ASAP. Send the cavalry."

Betty was right.

What circumstances had brought Stanford to this horrible scene? What happened and didn't happen? Coincidences and "what ifs"? Opportunities seized and missed? Cruel fate?

Justice achieved? You decide.

PART 1

1978

C H A P T E R   1

Two months earlier

The predator was slouched down in the front seat of his parked, gas-guzzling Buick Electra. It was an old, two-door model.

He was pissed off. He couldn't remember not being pissed off. *Why do they do this to me?* He repeated it over and over in his mind. These young *putas* drove him crazy.

The factory he worked at in Secaucus had closed down and moved south. He was a hi-lo operator, shifting full pallets of chemicals over to the loading dock. The job sucked, but he made decent money.

He thought something was up when he overheard the White bosses talking among themselves about moving to North Carolina. He knew they thought he was just a stupid spic who didn't *comprende* English. He encouraged that thinking, making them believe that he didn't understand much, as a ploy to find out inside information and avoid work whenever possible. But he was smarter than them, and he would show just how smart he was someday.

Now he was collecting unemployment benefits and, when the spirit moved him, making the shape for day labor "off the books."

There were certain street corners where men would gather in the mornings, hoping to be picked up for a day's work. Most of the guys were Salvadorians, Mexicans, Colombians, and "fucking Dominicans." Most of them were also illegal. When the landscapers and contractors pulled up with their trucks, these bastards would rush up and take the job for practically *nada*, screwing him. He was Puerto Rican, an American citizen, and these bastards were taking his bread.

Once in a while, when he thought he saw a fellow Boricua, he would flash his gang sign but never get a response. He had joined the Latin Kings when he was a teenager. He wasn't very active now, but this was a club you couldn't quit.

He had the three-pronged crown symbol tattooed on his biceps after undergoing the initiation process. It wasn't a complicated ceremony; they just encircled you and beat the shit out of you for as long as you could take it. He took it quite long, actually enjoying the beating. They praised his guts, not knowing that he found the warm, sweet taste of blood in his mouth quite pleasing.

This morning, he was in his favorite parking place in the high-rise lot, facing the adjoining elementary schoolyard. Oh, those sexy *chicas*! Just the way he liked them—nine or ten years old with no tits yet. They purposely wore short skirts to arouse him as they played tag and other games before they had to line up. Those naughty cunts really wanted it.

He adjusted the car mirrors so he could see if someone was coming up behind him. He then pulled the drawstring of his sweatpants, lowering them to his knees. He wore no underwear and began stroking his already hard penis. He quickly climaxed, pulled his sweats back up, and started the car.

He had stumbled upon this place by accident. St. Dominick's Church up the block ran a soup kitchen for the homeless and refugees. He dined with the good fathers occasionally, and they would be opening soon.

A perfect day—dinner and a show.

Paula Mahler felt like shit. She had been battling some kind of flu bug for a couple of days now. The over-the-counter remedies she was taking didn't work like they did in the TV commercials.

She had to be at work by 6:30 a.m. She was a clerk in the Horsemen's Bookkeeper office at the Meadowlands Racetrack in East Rutherford. At the track, all activities began early in the morning. Exercise riders worked thoroughbreds out at the crack of dawn. Hot walkers and grooms fed and bathed their charges. Owners and trainers made deposits or withdrawals in their accounts to enable them to buy and claim horses and pay bills.

She liked her job. It was an exciting atmosphere, sometimes meeting celebrities involved in the "sport of kings." She rented an apartment in the Lincoln Tower high-rise in West Hoboken. She didn't care much for the building or neighborhood. But at 6:00 a.m., she could jump right on Route 3 West and drive to the track in ten minutes. Usually.

This morning, as she approached the entrance ramp onto Route 3 West, she saw that traffic was severely backed up. Traffic in the other direction, Route 3 East, heading for the Lincoln Tunnel and midtown Manhattan, was also clogged. *Must be an accident,* she thought to herself. The thought made her head ache even more. She also then had chills and nausea.

"The hell with it," she said to herself, turning the car around and heading back home. "I'll call in sick and try to get an appointment with Dr. McDonald for later today."

This took far longer than expected because of the massive traffic congestion. Her nasal congestion was also massive at this point. She finally pulled into the building's parking lot and headed for her designated space near the rear. It was now almost 8:00 a.m.

"What the hell?" she exclaimed. There was an old car parked in her space. "Just what I need now." As she got closer, she saw there was a person seated behind the wheel. She blew the horn loudly and repeatedly.

Finally, a scruffy Hispanic man stuck his fat head out the driver's window, saying, "Sony, sorry, I got in the wrong spot." He started the car and pulled away, not to another spot but out of the lot.

She didn't recognize him, but she really didn't know many people in the building. She kept to herself, and there was a steady turnover of renters. She knew maybe five people to say hello to.

As she walked through the lot to the lobby, she thought she would complain to the concierge on duty at the front desk. At this time of day, it was Sammi Farush, an employee, who gave off an air of forced cordiality. As she neared the desk, Farush was busy helping an older woman with packages for her car. His smile was glimmering with the anticipation of a hefty tip.

I don't have time for this shit now, she thought. *It doesn't matter anyway. I just want to go lie down.*

But it did matter.

C H A P T E R   3

The usual morning routine of the Gomez family was progressing—badly.

The cramped, one-bedroom walkup was home to Elizer, the father, a foreman in a local embroidery factory; Maria, the mother, a seamstress; and two children, eleven-year-old Esmeralda and her six-year-old brother, Jesús.

Both children attended Webster Elementary School in downtown West Hoboken. Webster School was a large, old, overcrowded urban school, serving grades one through eight. It also housed special education classes, pre-K, and kindergarten. Bilingual and English as a Second Language classes had recently been added to all grades to try and cope with the large influx of students who recently emigrated from Central and South America. With almost two thousand students, Webster School was the largest in West Hoboken and possibly the state of New Jersey.

West Hoboken, like Webster School, was also old and overcrowded. It was a densely populated town with a listed population of over fifty-five thousand but an actual population of close to seventy-five thousand due to illegal apartments hidden in basements and attics. These were rented out to undocumented aliens at exorbitant prices.

The Gomez family was atypical of this situation: hardworking, religious, legal immigrants from the Dominican Republic. Every morning, the four members of the family raced to eat breakfast, use the tiny bathroom, dress, and get out on time to work or school. It usually doesn't work out this way, though, and today was no exception.

"Papi, Papi," Esmi cried, "Jesus is too slow. We're going to be late again."

"Esmi, you know how Mama and I have to leave first so we can earn the money to buy you those delicious *arepas* you are eating for breakfast," Elizer said lovingly as he patted her head.

"But, Papi, when we miss the lineup, I have to walk Jesus to his class, and his teacher yells at me! She's mean and says I have to get him here on time, and then I have to go upstairs to my classroom, and my teacher yells at me and says I'll never amount to anything," she sulked.

"No, no, no, that's not true, *mi linda*. You are smart and pretty and can become anything you want," her father continued. "That's why we came to America because there are opportunities here if you work hard and worship God. Now *andale*. Put on your pretty red dress and go," he ordered.

"Aw, Papi, that dress is old-fashioned. The other girls make fun of me," she implored.

"No, it is a proper dress for a girl your age. Do not pay attention to them. They are not good Christians," he replied.

Finally, at 8:30 a.m., Esmi dragged Jesús down the three flights of stairs out to Summit Avenue and headed out. Since they were already fifteen minutes late, Esmi correctly figured that the lines had gone inside the building and were probably halfway through the Pledge of Allegiance and the morning announcements.

She decided to take a shortcut through the Lincoln Towers high-rise parking lot. That cut several blocks of the trip, rather than walk all the way around the large residential complex.

The parking lot was backed up against the north schoolyard. There was a gap in the cyclone fence that allowed them to squeeze through and step into the side door of the school.

They had done it several times and gotten away with it.

On this day, they did not.

CHAPTER 4

Maria Gomez was riding on the number 22 public service bus return-ing home. Her mind was numb with the mundane events of the day. She had worked her usual eight-hour shift at the Apex Embroidery factory in Hoboken. They mainly manufactured high-end table-cloths for rich people.

She sewed applique flowers to the large tablecloths all day long. She was on her feet constantly, and those dogs were barking. Her hands were sore from cutting the flowers from the completed sheets with large shears.

Sitting on the bus seat next to her was a large bag of sheets, which she was taking home to cut and prepare for tomorrow's work. This "piece work," as it was called, provided a little extra income for the family.

The hoagie she had eaten for lunch was repeating on her as the bus bumped along. She really didn't like the cold-cut sandwiches they were given, but they were free. Mr. Murphy, the kindly manager, had arranged with a caterer to bring in lunch daily at no cost to the staff.

The two older Italian men who prepared and delivered the food were suspicious-looking characters. She didn't like them. The one with the glass eye always leered at her breasts and called her sweet-heart as he served the food. But the kids loved the heroes, and she was usually able to sneak one or two home.

Maria got off at her usual stop and trudged three blocks to her apartment. She couldn't wait to get home and put her feet up for a little while, but she would have to get dinner started soon. Her hus-band would be coming home and insisted on eating as a family at 6 o'clock sharp.

She opened the outside door with her key and ascended the three flights to the apartment. She had a strange feeling as she neared the top floor and realized it was the sounds emanating from the home. There were none.

Usually, the television would be blasting, or Esmi would be yelling at Jesus to keep quiet so she could do her homework, but nothing.

She entered the railroad flat in eerie silence. The snack she always left out for the kids was untouched. A chill went up her spine. This had never happened before. Where were they? What should she do?

She went downstairs to the insurance agent's office on the ground floor.

"Mr. Davino, have you seen the children today?" she asked. He was the owner, and he was closing up for the day.

"No, I didn't see them today. They usually wave to me when they come in," he added.

She bolted outside, running wildly up and down the street, calling, "Esmi, Jesus! Esmi, where are you?"

Maybe they went to a friend's house after school, she hoped. No, she reconsidered. They really didn't have any friends here. The other kids didn't like them because her husband was so strict with them.

All day Saturday was spent at church. It was too much. They had no freedom, no fun. They should be playing with the other kids on Saturdays. She would always tell Elizer that he had to loosen up on them. Now she was in a cold sweat.

"Elizer will be home soon. He will know what to do, I hope," she said to herself, then added, "Mary, Mother of God, please help me."

CHAPTER 5

Detective Shack sat back in his chair, his big feet up on the desk, digesting the linguine with clam sauce he had just devoured—for free—across the street at the Town Hall Tavern. They made a mean white clam sauce, and you couldn't beat the price. He and his partner were working an eight-hour shift that day, from noon to 8:00 p.m.

Chief Brown was experimenting with shift times for detectives while keeping the Uniform Division in the traditional mode. Uniforms had three eight-hour shifts, "straight days," from 8:00 a.m. to 4:00 p.m.; "nights," from 4:00 p.m. to midnight; and "graveyard," from midnight to 8:00 a.m. Detectives were rarely needed at the graveyard, so he was saturating straight days and nights until then with senior officers.

This was fine with Shack. He didn't have to get up early, and by the time he clocked out at 8:00 p.m., he didn't have to spend much time at home with his wife. A win-win situation. Thus he took his meal around 6:00 p.m., usually across the street, because for cops, it was on the house.

His partner, Detective Smith, returned to the Detective Bureau and summoned Shack. "C'mon, we have to see Charley downstairs."

Captain Charley Corales was the night commander of the Uniform Division and bagman for the bosses. In between shaking down the many taverns and gambling operations in town, he would let in a little police work.

As the pair of detectives went into Corales's office, he whined in his high-pitched voice, "Two missing Spanish kids downtown. We did a preliminary search, but nothing. The parents say they're good kids," he continued.

"Yeah, all these PRs are good kids," Shack replied. They collected the contact information and made their way to their unmarked car.

"This will work out perfectly," Shack said to his partner. "It's like 7:30 now. We can go down there and drag it out into a couple hours of overtime," he continued, grinning greedily.

Driving down to the Gomezes' apartment with Smith at the wheel, Shack recalled, "Aw, Rickie, you shoulda come with me. That clam sauce was unreal."

"I can see you enjoyed it. You're wearing it well," Smith replied sarcastically.

Shack glanced down and saw that his cheap clip-on tie was covered in greasy clam sauce spots. I'll just throw it away after the interview, he thought to himself. He had a large collection of clip-ons at home.

That's all he ever wore, having learned the hard way when, as a young detective, a drunk pounded his face while choking him with his real tie.

"You'll make a good impression on those parents with that tie," Smith chuckled.

"Aw, Rickie, you know the way this is gonna go. Some ex-husband, aunt, or abuela picked up the kids from school and forgot to tell the parents. Their families are huge. They can't keep track of all these kids," he ranted, racism showing through his words.

But it didn't go that way.

The two lumbering detectives entered the small apartment after climbing the three flights of stairs. Detective Shack's deodorant was losing the battle of "all-day freshness." He was the type of guy that if you had to spend any amount of time with, you would want to take a shower.

"So, Mr. Gomez, have the kids ever run away before?" Shack began.

"Absolutely not," Elizer replied. "They would never do that. They understand to come straight home from school, do their homework, and wait for their mother to come home at five o'clock." His face reddened with anger.

"Well, sometimes these kids go to their friends' house, the park, or something," Shack continued.

"These kids would not," Elizer retorted tensely, cutting off the detective's monologue. He was rapidly losing faith in the abilities of American law enforcement.

Detective Smith noticed the mother standing quietly behind her husband. He was doing all the talking. Occasionally, she would nod in agreement. There was no question about who was in charge in this household.

"We went to the school as soon as I got home," the father continued, "but it was all locked up. Nobody was around."

"Yeah, we'll go over there tomorrow and check things out. See if the teachers or the kids might know something," Shack continued.

"You must do something now!" Elizer shouted, pounding his fist on the kitchen table.

"Whoa, take it easy, *amigo*. We already put out an APB with Uniform Patrol. They're combing every street in town," Shack reassured him.

Detective Smith added, "Sir, the last time something like this occurred, the kids had played hooky and took the bus up to Palisades Amusement Park. They were afraid to come home, so they hid out. Don't worry, we'll find them."

As they left the apartment, Shack turned to Smith. "C'mon, let's go back to HQ and type up a report. That'll give us a couple extra hours of OT. We'll go to school tomorrow at the start of the shift, at noon. That is, if they haven't come home already."

But they hadn't gone to any amusement parks.

A red-faced Captain O'Brien stopped Shack at the door of the police station.

"Don't even come in. Get down to Webster School and the Gomezes' place. Those kids didn't come home last night. The father's been calling the mayor, that prick Artie Cortez at the newspaper, everybody." Gasping for breath, he continued, "I'm going to give you some help, but get going now."

Shack picked up Smith, and the two sped down to Webster School. They entered the front door and went directly to the principal's office on the first floor.

The principal, Frank Woods, welcomed them into his unit office. "What can I do for you, detectives?" he asked with a cheesy smile.

"Two of your kids didn't come home from school yesterday," Smith began. Woods's smile vanished, and his face paled.

"What are their names?" Woods queried.

"Esmeralda and Jesus Gomez. She's in Miss Albreckt's fifth-grade class, and Jesus is in Mrs. Jones's first grade. We'd like to go up and talk to the teachers," Smith continued.

"Sure, sure, I'll go with you," Woods said as the two left his office. "Mrs. Jones's class is right around the corner."

As with most elementary schools, the lower grades were on the first floor and the older kids on the second and third floors. Mrs. Jones was quizzing the class about alphabet sounds when she saw the men and stepped out into the hallway, casting an authoritative glance at the students to silence them.

"Mrs. Jones, I'd like to see Jesus Gomez. Is he here today?" Woods asked.

"I'd like to see him too, Mr. Woods, but he's absent today."

"Oh, these men are police. It seems Jesus didn't come home from school yesterday," Woods continued nervously. "Who picked him up?"

"Yesterday? Nobody picked him up. He was absent yesterday, too. His older sister usually comes for him, but he was out. I sent the attendance record to the office," she said defensively.

"How is he as a student?" Detective Smith asked.

"Average ability. He's very quiet, doesn't participate much, and is chronically late, although these are his first two absences all year."

Shack, sensing this was going nowhere, thanked the teacher and said, "Let's go up to the girl's class. The fact that Jesus hadn't made it to school at all yesterday changed things for the worse."

They went to the second-floor fifth-grade classroom of Ms. Albreckt. She looked just like the grumpy teacher in the *Our Gang* movies.

Woods tried again. "Ms. Albreckt, is Esmi Gomez in class today?"

"No, she was absent yesterday and today," the teacher responded curtly, as if each word she spoke cost her money. "I notified the office. I'll show you her attendance card."

Detective Shack scanned the attendance card and said, "I see she's only been out these past two days, but she's late a lot."

"Thirty-four times tardy since September," she muttered, shaking her head.

Tardy, Smith thought to himself, *I haven't heard that word in years.*

Woods jumped in. "How is she in class?"

"She's quiet, secretive, below average in reading and math level, and, of course, displays uncooperative behavior with her tardiness," she added.

"How are the parents?" Shack asked.

"I never saw the mother. Father came for Parent Night and had a defensive attitude."

"Does she have any close friends in the class?" Smith asked.

"I wouldn't know. I don't get involved in that nonsense. I really have to get back to teaching now. They just can't seem to grasp declarative sentences." She turned on her sensible heels and was gone.

Frustrated, Shack entered the room behind her and bellowed to the class, "Did anyone see Esmi yesterday or today?" A wall of silence and blank faces looked back at him.

He quickly stormed out, collected Smith, thanked Woods for the "great help" he and his staff had been, and left the school.

"Let's get over to the Gomezes' apartment," Smith said.

"Yeah. Before we do, Rickie, I want to run something by you," Shack replied.

Smith nodded. "Go ahead."

"I'm starting to like the father for this," Shack blurted out.

"Aw, Vic, no," Smith started.

"No, listen, listen, Rickie. The kids fit the perfect profile of abused children: quiet, an issue with hiding something, secretive. The father acted all upset, but the mother, not so much. He's way too affectionate in the way he talks about Esmi like she's his wife, not his daughter. She's so good. She's so beautiful. She would never do anything wrong."

"I think you see something that isn't there," Smith replied. "Besides, the timing's wrong. The father leaves first, then the mother, then the kids. When's the opportunity?"

"What if the father leaves, hides out somewhere, waits for the mother to leave, then goes back for the girl?" Shack thought.

"No, I don't agree, and where does the little boy fit in?" Smith asked.

"Collateral damage," Shack spat out. "Let's go see if the father has an alibi for yesterday morning."

This ought to go over great, Smith thought to himself as they drove over to the Gomezes' apartment.

It was about two o'clock by the time they got to the Gomezes' place. Both parents were sitting at the kitchen table, praying. It looked like neither one had slept.

Shack began, "We were over at the school. It turned out the kids didn't show up at all yesterday. The teacher said Esmi was quiet and secretive like she was hiding something. Do you know what that could be, Mr. Gomez?"

"No, I don't. We teach her to be respectful in school. She's mature and doesn't chatter about like the silly young girls," Gomez answered.

"What about you, Mrs. Gomez? Is there anything Esmi might want to get away from here?" Shack asked.

"No, what do you mean?" Maria answered, confused.

"Mr. Gomez, where were you yesterday morning?" Shack went on aggressively.

"Why, I left here around 7:30 and walked to work. I open up the factory at 8:00," Gomez replied with an edge in his voice.

"Can anyone vouch for your whereabouts?" Shack kept pushing.

"Yes, thirty of my workers, you evildoer. Do you think I could hurt my daughter, my love? Get out of my house right now!" yelling at the top of his lungs.

Smith jumped in and tried to calm him. "We have to ask these questions to the family. It's routine procedure." He added, "Is there anyone you know who would want to hurt the kids? Do you have any enemies?"

Gomez said, "Yes, there is. But get him out of here right now. I can't bear to look at his black soul."

Smith nodded to Shack to leave, and he went on. "Who are you talking about?"

"Mario Alonso. He belongs to my church. He was our elder, but the congregation was unhappy with him. He was lazy. We had an election for the elder. I won, and he swore revenge upon me."

Smith gathered Alonso's contact information and left, briskly telling Gomez, "We'll get right on this." But Gomez was already busy calling Captain O'Brien to complain about Shack and paid no attention to him.

They returned to the Detective Bureau and encountered a furious Captain O'Brien. They verbally gave him the cliff notes version of the interviews of the morning.

"Write up the reports right now, and stay here. I'll send somebody else to interview Alonso. You've done enough damage for one day." As the words left O'Brien's mouth, a call came in summoning him to the Mayor's Office.

O'Brien trudged up the stairs to the Mayor's Office and gave the angry Corso a progress report on the investigation, or rather, a lack of progress report.

"Wilbur, I'm getting calls from the father, the entire church congregation, and that prick Artie Cortez from the *Jersey Journal* is killing me, and you have these two morons handling the case? Who are your best detectives?" Corso demanded.

"Well, John Pinto is my best man, but you wanted him detailed to the Commissioner's Office to handle special cases," O'Brien replied meekly.

"You mean he's fixing parking tickets and DWI's for our loyal supporters," Corso said.

"Yeah, pretty much," O'Brien answered.

"Well, get him on the case. I'll tell Commissioner Johnson we need him. And get Billy Stanford involved. He knows the school system. Those idiots got nothing out of the staff. Billy knows how to talk to those people. I'll tell Johnson I want him involved too."

And that was the first step that led Stanford to that godforsaken riverbank.

CHAPTER 9

Detective John Pinto and Bill Stanford headed downtown, as per Mayor Corso's orders, to try to salvage this case.

"John, how about you go over to the Gomezes' apartment and talk to the parents? Drop me at Webster School. I'll talk to the teachers."

"Good idea," Pinto replied. Although Italian-American, Pinto had become totally fluent in Spanish in his twenty years as a detective. He could smooth over feelings with the family and possibly get more information than the crude Detective Shack.

Stanford, being in the school system and known as Mayor Corso's "golden boy," figured he could get better cooperation from the school officials, as he had actually worked at Webster School for a short time.

While Detective Pinto was meeting with the Gomezes', Stanford stopped at Principal Woods's office. He knew Frank Woods for many years. He was a good man, but he was counting down the days until his retirement. His assistant principal, Josh Conforti, was doing the same. Neither were really involved with the children or parents anymore.

Stanford bypassed Mrs. Jones, Jesus's teacher. He didn't know her at all, and he thought the older sister's class might be a better bet. Plus, he knew Ms. Albreckt, the old battle-ax teacher, who he surprisingly got along with when he taught there.

"Hello, Marie," Stanford greeted Ms. Albreckt outside her classroom, using her first name. Something nobody dared to do.

She smiled at the handsome, much younger man, greeting him warmly and saying, "I hear you're doing alright for yourself since you left us here."

"I learned it all from you," he countered with his roguish Irish grin. He went on, his white teeth dazzling. "That's kind of why I'm here, Marie. I'm helping the police with these missing children."

"Yes, a terrible thing, Bill, but I really don't know much about her or the family," she answered.

"Does she have any friends at all in the class?" he asked.

"You know, I don't have any idea about that, Bill. But you're welcome to talk to the class."

"That would be great," he answered, adding, "Take a little break in the teacher's room. I'll come get you when I finish." He knew she was probably dying for a cigarette, as she was a heavy smoker.

Stanford entered the class and explained that he needed their help finding Esmi. Any little thing they might know could help bring her safely home. One little dark-skinned girl at the back was looking like she wanted to say something but was holding back. He thanked them, took note of her seat position, and retrieved Ms. Albreckt.

"Marie, who's the little girl at the last seat in the back, second row?" he asked, trying not to breathe in the secondhand smoke wafting off her breath and clothes.

"Oh, that's Caridad Sofia. She's new, from the Dominican Republic, and very shy."

"Yeah, I see that. Do me a favor and send her out in the hall to me."

Albreckt did so, and he questioned the girl gently, alone in the hall. "Caridad, I know you wanted to tell me something in there," Stanford began. "Please, help me."

Caridad's lip trembled as she fought back tears. "I don't want to get in trouble. She's nice to me."

"Caridad, I won't tell Ms. Albreckt or anybody else. What is it?"

Softly, she replied, "She and Jesus are late a lot, and Ms. Albreckt yells at them, so they take a shortcut through the parking lot into the schoolyard where we line up. Will that help?" she asked.

"Oh, yes, Caridad," he replied solemnly, "that will help very much."

Stanford exited Webster School by the side door and walked to the back of the schoolyard, where the fence cordoned off the Lincoln Towers parking lot. Sure enough, there was a gap in the fence. It was too small for him to squeeze his muscular, 210-pound frame through, but certainly doable for a skinny, eleven-year-old girl and a five-year-old boy.

He called Detective Pinto on his WHPD-issued walkie-talkie. Pinto was wrapping up his interview with the parents and told him to meet him at the car parked near the apartment. Stanford informed him of the fence situation and his reluctant informant, Caridad.

"John, what do you think of the father?" Stanford asked.

"He's a bit of a religious fanatic but no killer. He wouldn't hurt his children. He's convinced this Mario Alonso guy from the church is our man," he said. "I'll drop you back at school and go interrogate him. I got an address from the father. I want it to be official, so I'll do it myself. The courts might frown on a civilian being present at an official questioning of a person of interest," he continued. "I'll bring Boylen to go with me as backup."

"No *problemo*. I don't want to screw anything up," Stanford said. "I'll meet you back at city hall after school. You can fill me in then."

Stanford went back and taught a few history classes, his mind wandering from the 1948 presidential election to what was happening now in real life. His duties were flexible, as he was in charge of a work-study program in which he left the school early to supervise students working in the area. He also taught several US history classes each day.

Pinto picked up Detective Tom Boylen at WHPD and went to interview Mario Alonso. Boylen was another veteran detective, smart and with an imposing physical presence. They would double-team him.

At about 3:30, Pinto returned and met with Stanford. "Alonso's clean, with an ironclad alibi. He was out of the country on March 20. He just got back. I checked his passport." He went on, "He travels a lot for business, more so lately. That's why the father thinks he's lazy in his church activities. He is just making a living," he said. "Dead end."

"Shit," Stanford replied. "Now what?"

"Let's go brief Captain O'Brien and the commissioner on our findings," Pinto said.

"Yeah, that'll be fun. Maybe the mayor will join us too," Stanford replied sarcastically.

After hearing their report, Captain O'Brien said, "Well, at least this fence shortcut might be a lead. Get a group of men tomorrow, early, and flood the area. Check with Lincoln Towers; question all people leaving around that time. Maybe somebody saw something in the lot.

"And Billy, contact that prick Artie Cortez of the *Jersey Journal* and get the kids' pictures in the paper. Talk to the *Hudson Dispatch* too. And see if you can get some of the TV stations involved."

Stanford agreed and immediately started calling his newspaper contacts. He gave Artie Cortez the information about the fence shortcut and informed him that it looked like the kids were grabbed in that area on their way to school. He could make it on the front-page news in the next edition by scooping the *Dispatch*, the rival daily paper.

He then called the New York TV stations ABC-7, NBC-4, and CBS-2, as well as the local stations WOR and WPIX. They responded with lukewarm interest, but he would keep pushing.

All this took several hours, and when he looked up, it was seven o'clock, and he was exhausted. He went home hoping that all this might help in some way, along with tomorrow's dragnet of the area.

But it didn't.

The next morning, Detectives Boylen, Smith, Pinto, and Shack were joined by several uniformed officers in stopping everyone in the area and showing pictures of the missing children.

They spoke to Farush, the security man in the Lincoln Towers, asking him if there had been any problems in the parking lot. He answered honestly, no.

That was because Paula Mahler had never bothered to report her encounter with the scruffy man in her parking spot two months ago. At this time in the morning at eight, she was on her second cup of coffee at her desk at the Meadowlands Racetrack. Therefore, she missed all the police activity going on in her lobby and parking lot.

Some of the detectives went door-to-door along the route the children would have taken to school. *Nada.* One nice lady told them, "Officers, we see a hundred kids that look like the picture go by every morning." That pretty much summed up most of the comments they received. After several hours, they had zilch to show for their efforts and left.

Stanford got a call hours later in the day from Joan Montgomery, the beautiful, blonde anchor from Channel 7 *Eyewitness News.* They had a nice conversation, and she promised to get something on that evening's broadcast.

He was surprised that she had called him herself, not some intern or producer. Maybe she did like him. He was trying to talk her into coming over and doing a standup shot onsite. She was a babe.

Over the next week or so, the newspapers and TV news stations played up the disappearance big, but nothing of importance was discovered.

While all this fruitless activity was taking place in Hudson County, the killer was simultaneously motoring westward in his beat-up Buick. He had fled the scene of the crime, jumping on Route 80 West and deciding to drive to California. He had a duffle bag in the backseat with all his meager belongings. He kept it there because he was several weeks behind on his rent at the fleabag residential hotel where he had been staying. Eventually, he figured, they would kick him out.

As he drove, his brain pulsated, going over the events of the day. Why didn't that little boy let go of her hand and run like she told him? Why did he get in the car with them? "I didn't want to hurt him. He was a boy." Raping and killing the girl was not a concern for him, however. "That bitch was asking for it—the way she kept teasing me for months. Then when I gave her what she wanted, she fought me and tried to scratch my eyes."

Perez had some heavy packing cords in the car, which he had stolen from the factory. He used it to tie her hands so he could take his time and enjoy her.

As he drove, he kept punching the three preset buttons on his AM radio. He had to find the song he loved. They played it all the time; it was number one. *It was like his theme song*, he thought.

Finally, on WMCA 570, "Home of the Good Guys," he found it in progress.

You're no good; you're no good; baby, you're no good. He sang along with Linda something, the chick who had made the record. *She was kinda hot-looking*, he thought, *for an older woman*. He mentally dedicated the song to Esmi and all the young girls who purposely drove him crazy.

The other stations would play it soon, he knew: WABC 770 with Cousin Brucie and 1010 WINS with Murray the K. They all played the same top 40 songs over and over.

The music calmed him as he drove. However, the car wasn't running smoothly. *Maybe I should have changed the oil last year when the guy told me*, he thought. The wheels were shaking badly when he went over 60 mph. The guy had said something about wheel alignments being needed.

"Aw, fuck it," he concluded, turning up the volume.

You're no good; you're no good; you're no good; baby, you're no good.

CHAPTER 12

Later that night, as William Albert Perez drove along Route 80, the car was shaking badly, and the engine sputtered. A loud *crack* emitted from under the hood, and Perez smelled smoke. He pulled over to the shoulder as he saw flames come out of the hood. He grabbed his duffel bag and got out as another explosion rocked the car. The entire car was engulfed in flames within a minute.

He started walking along the highway. He wasn't sure exactly where he was. After a few miles, a truck pulled over, offering him a ride to the next rest area. The driver asked, "Was that your car on fire back there?"

"Yes," he answered.

"Sounds like it's totaled," the driver said.

"Yes," he answered.

The driver pulled into the rest area, letting him out. "Good luck," he said.

"Yes," Perez answered.

He entered a Howard Johnson's restaurant, his bag slung over his shoulder. A "HELP WANTED" sign was in the front window. He sat at the counter and ordered a cup of coffee. "You lookin' for help?" he asked the counterman.

"Yes, we need a dishwasher."

"I can do that," Perez answered.

"I'll get the manager. He's in the back."

The manager talked to him briefly, explaining the pay, hours, and benefits, the latter of which were none. "When can you start?" he ended.

"Now," Perez replied, getting up and heading for the kitchen.

"You have a place to stay?" the manager asked, eyeing his duffel bag.

"No."

"We have a room at the back the guys share. We're open for twenty-four hours. They sleep and work in shifts. You can work it out with them."

Perez stayed for several weeks. The pay was low, but he had plenty to eat. The room was a shithole, but he wouldn't be there much longer. It turned out that he was in western Pennsylvania, not far from the Penn National Race Course. He had been a groom in Puerto Rico and was interested in getting a job there. The longer he stayed away from New Jersey, the better it was to let things cool off.

He took a bus to the Penn National Race Course and was hired as a groom. He had a bed in the dormitory and a meal pass for the cafeteria. He liked it better than the Howard Johnson and stayed for several months.

After being on the road for six months, Perez decided to return to Hudson County. Enough time had passed, and he was feeling strong urges again. He had seen some pretty young girls eyeing him up at the restaurant and track, but he didn't act on it. It was getting harder and harder for him to control himself. He would feel more comfortable back in New Jersey, where he knew the streets and alleys.

"Yeah, it's time to go home."

Perez took a series of buses and arrived at the apartment of his second cousin, Gladys Orozco, unannounced. She lived in Hoboken and was a single mother with a ten-year-old daughter, Matilda.

"Gladys, *como estas?*" Perez greeted her on her front porch, or stoop, as it was called in this area.

"Oh, William, good to see you," she responded half-heartedly. All his friends and family called him William, never Willie. "I haven't seen you in a while. Where have you been?"

"My factory closed. I went out of town to find work, but I couldn't stay away for long." He leered at her daughter Matilda, who had joined them on the stoop. "Gladys, do me a favor. I just need a place to stay for a few nights until I find work."

"William, the apartment is really small. There's not much room," she responded calmly, not crazy about this idea.

"Aw, please?" he begged. "Just a few nights. I'll be out all day looking for work and my own place. I've got some leads for work. I gotta see some people."

"Alright. You'll have to sleep on the couch. There's only one bedroom, and Matilda and I share it."

"Oh, God bless you, Gladys. Thank you so much. You won't be sorry."

But she would be very sorry.

As a few nights dragged on into a few weeks, tension built between William and Gladys.

"William, you said you had jobs lined up. What happened?" she demanded one evening.

"Bad luck, Gladys, but I couldn't get anything. I'm sorry."

You're sorry, Gladys thought to herself. *I'm sorry that I said yes.*

"There's an old saying in Puerto Rico, William. Company is like fish. After three days, it starts to stink."

"Okay, okay. I'll leave soon," he said.

"Please, William. I can't afford you. You eat like a horse. I'm broke. I have to go to Rite-Aid now and get some medicine for Matilda. She's sick and can't go to school today. She has a fever. I'll be right back."

"Take your time, Gladys. I'll take care of her."

As soon as Gladys left, Perez slipped into Matilda's bedroom. He took a cold washcloth with him.

"Matilda, here, put this on your head. Mama said you have a fever." He had been having strong urges since the first day he had seen her. This was his chance. He patted her head soothingly with the cold cloth.

At first, it felt good to the young girl, but then he started moving down her body with the cloth. She became scared. "*Tio, Tio,* stop. Don't touch me there."

"Matilda, just relax. You're making your fever worse. Just lay there quietly."

"No, no," she started screaming. Matilda was ten, but she knew what was going on here.

After a few minutes, Perez was so sexually aroused that he didn't hear the front door open. Gladys heard Matilda screaming in the bedroom. She threw open the door and saw Perez fondling her daughter with his penis exposed.

"You son of a bitch! Son of a bitch!" she screamed as loudly as she could, and she had a strong voice.

The next-door neighbor heard the screams through their paper-thin walls and called the police. Gladys ran to the kitchen and picked up the still-hot frying pan that she used to fry up some plantains for breakfast.

She swung away at Perez, landing some good shots to the head and face. He screamed. The combination of the heavy pan and hot grease caused him severe pain. All the while, she kept screaming, "You son of a bitch!"

The Hoboken Police arrived shortly thereafter, briefly sized up the scene, and took Perez into custody.

"Please calm down, Mrs. Orozco. Our detective will be here soon to speak to you and your daughter. Don't change clothes or bathe her until they get her. This is a severe crime, and we have to follow certain rules."

The uniformed policeman was experienced and calm, and Gladys saw he knew what he was doing.

"Another patrolman is going to take him to jail. The detectives will be here any minute. My partner and I will stay with you here until they arrive."

She hugged him and started crying, her anger having melted into sorrow. She then hugged Matilda, who was also now crying profusely.

Detectives Antonelli and Conde of Hoboken PD arrived and took the report from the uniforms in a professional manner. Thus the case against William Albert Perez began.

CHAPTER 14

Detective Frank Antonelli showed up back at the police station and instructed the patrolman to bring William Albert Perez to the downstairs interrogation room.

This room differed from the upstairs official interrogation room, as it had no two-way mirrors, cameras, or tape recorders. It was used for special cases such as this.

Antonelli was nearing retirement age and was sick of dealing with scum like Perez. It seemed to him that these types of sex crimes were becoming more prevalent as he got older. Or maybe his tolerance for these perverts was exhausted. One way or another, he was going to put this creep away for a long time. He already had him dead to rights for attempted rape of a minor and several related charges like illegal touching, assault, and exposing himself.

But Antonelli was experienced and knew that a monster like Perez didn't wake up this morning at the age of twenty-eight and decide to become a child molester. He was sure he had committed or attempted to commit other crimes of this caliber. It usually started with peeping or exposing himself and progressed into sexual contact. With the right questioning techniques, he could probably close a lot of open cases in which Perez was the perp.

Perez was handcuffed to the single chair bolted to the floor opposite the plain desk and chair Antonelli and Conde sat at. Antonelli took the lead.

"So, William. I hope you don't have any plans for the next thirty years because you are going away to Trenton State really soon." He punctured this statement with a backhanded whack across his bruised and burned face with a rolled-up telephone book, his tool of choice for "difficult" suspects. He liked the phone book because it hurt the perp but didn't bruise or cut his hands, providing no evidence of police brutality. These bleeding-heart liberals didn't understand what it took to get information from these miscreants.

"Who else did you touch, William?"

"Nobody."

Thwack. Thwack. A forehand and backhand that Rod Laver would be proud of followed.

"Wrong answer, William. Let's try again." *Thwack.* "Where were you before you stayed with your cousin?"

"I was out of town. I lost my job in Secaucus, and I was looking for work," Perez mumbled through bleeding lips.

"What town?" Antonelli raised the phone book, but before he could strike again, Perez answered.

"I worked at Howard Johnson near Harrisburg and the racetrack in Grantville. You can check. I'm clean."

"I *will* check, scumbag. Where did you live when you were here?"

"Hotel Alberty in West Hoboken," he answered.

"What was the name of the factory you worked at in Secaucus?"

"Onyx Chemical. They moved to North Carolina," Perez answered, now trying to come off as cooperative so this guy would stop hitting him. His forehead was killing him, especially the burns from the hot grease.

Detective Conde, who had been silent until now, spoke up. "Have you ever been convicted of a crime or been arrested for a crime? We have your fingerprints from your booking, and we are comparing them now as we speak to several open cases. It would be best if you told us now."

Conde was attempting the good guy role, which, in truth, he was. Younger than Antonelli, he didn't approve of his mentor's tactics at times, and he didn't particularly like him as a person, but he closed a lot of cases.

"No, no, I didn't do anything to anybody," Perez whined. "My niece was showing off her body. She wanted it."

That remark infuriated Antonelli, and he brushed by Conde, grabbing Perez by both ears and pressing his thumbs into the burns on his forehead and cheeks. Perez screamed in pain as Conde recoiled.

"If you don't have the stomach for this, get out, Conde!" Antonelli yelled. "Don't come back until you grow some balls!" Antonelli didn't much care for his young Hispanic partner, who was promoted due to affirmative action, not ability.

"You're nuts," Conde said and left.

"Okay now, William. It's just the two of us."

Bang-Whack. Perez's one eye was swelling shut, and he was bleeding from the nose and mouth. The burns were getting darker and blistering. This guy can take it, Antonelli thought to himself as he kneaded him in the groin several times. "I'll fix you so you'll never hurt another little girl or little boy."

"I would never hurt a boy. Boys are good. The young girls are sluts." Another knee connected with his stomach.

"Oh," Perez gasped as the wind left his lungs. "I told you I didn't hurt the boy. He was in the water. It was his bitch sister's fault."

Something in this scenario sounded familiar to Antonelli, so he paused in his assault and thought for a while. He had an encyclopedic memory of crimes that the other detectives had kidded him about but admired.

Then it hit him. The kidnapped brother and sister from West Hoboken—they were found murdered near an abandoned factory in Secaucus, on the Hackensack River, some seven months ago. The time fit. He would bet the closed factory was going to turn out to be the Onyx Co., where Perez had worked.

It was time to call his friend Wilber O'Brien, the chief of detectives up in West Hoboken. He should meet this guy. Right now.

CHAPTER 15

Captain O'Brien raced down to Hoboken, taking Detective John Pinto with him. He had known Frank Antonelli for many years, and if he thought this Perez was the guy, he was probably right. You could say a lot of things about Antonelli, but he was a smart cop.

O'Brien and Pinto joined Antonelli in the dungeon-like room in the basement. They were shocked at Perez's appearance. His face was one mass of swollen flesh. Not that they had any sympathy for him, but a confession after a beating like this would create some legal problems.

"Jeez, Frank, you did some job on him," O'Brien commented. "But I think you're right. He's our guy. The factory he worked at, Onyx, was near where the bodies were found. And he didn't kill the little boy. The boy drowned. Nobody knew that except the killer. We kept that from the press."

"Did you Miranda him, Frank?" O'Brien asked.

"Oh, yes, several times," Antonelli lied as he smacked the rolled-up phone book in his palm.

"Where is his car?" Pinto asked, thinking some forensic evidence might be able to salvage this case.

"He claims it burned up on the highway near Harrisburg. You guys could check that out."

"Did he ask for a lawyer?" Pinto continued.

"No, he talked to us freely." Antonelli lied again, hoping that chicken-shit Conde would back him up.

"How did his face get like that?" O'Brien asked.

"His cousin Gladys hit him with a hot frying pan. Tough woman." Antonelli laughed. "He deserved it. They should give her a medal."

"Is the girl alright?" Pinto asked.

"Yeah, shaken up, of course, but the mother got back unexpectedly and stopped it before he could get too far. We have him on several counts. However, you guys could get him for murder."

"I'd like to take him up to our shop and do just that, Frank. Is there any problem with that?"

"No *problemo*. Wilber, this piece of shit is all yours. We'll defer our charges while you try to build a murder case."

O'Brien's mind was racing. He would have to call the county prosecutor and get a public defender to go through the motions with Perez. His face would be a problem. Lack of forensics would be a problem. The confession was tainted. Still, he was glad they had this guy off the streets. There would have to be some creative maneuvering, but he had some ideas already. Pinto would help him; he was "creative" too.

He called ahead to West Hoboken PD and asked for the holding cell to be emptied. He also called Monica Cervalli, a public defender who owed him a favor. Then he called Harold Gardner, the Hudson County prosecutor, who he could also work with.

This just might work out. The politicians will be happy. Mayor Corso and Commissioner Johnson could help out with those bothersome rules they slipped up on. But in the end, he thought justice just might prevail.

C H A P T E R   1 6

William Albert Perez was arraigned in West Hoboken Municipal Court, charged with two counts of kidnapping, the murder and rape of Esmi, and reckless endangerment causing the death of little Jesus.

All the New York TV stations sent talking heads—Gabe Pressman from NBC-4, Linda Ellerbee from CBS 2, Marvin Scott from WPIX 11, and Bill Stanford's favorite, Joan Montgomery of WABC Eyewitness News.

Stanford invited Montgomery to lunch across the street at the Town Hall Tavern. She went, hoping for some information she could use to scoop up the other stations. She knew Stanford liked her and was playing him like a violin. She hated the Town Hall Tavern and the food, hardly touching it. She extracted some exclusives from him and made a hasty exit, telling him she had to get back to the station.

Stanford went back across the street to the police station and joined a strategy session with Captain O'Brien and others. Perez was transported to the Hudson County Jail in Jersey City to be held, awaiting trial without bail.

O'Brien explained that County Prosecutor Gardner was going to try to negotiate a plea deal with the public defender. They did not want to take this to trial. There were too many problems. The car was burned to a crisp, destroying all forensic evidence. The shell was then compacted and shipped to China for scrap metal. Perez's confession was tainted by the beating. Several procedural errors were made. There was no doubt Perez was guilty, however.

Public Defender Cavelli, looking for a prosecutor's job in the near future, talked Perez into pleading guilty by reason of insanity and accepting a life sentence in the Mountain View Mental Hospital for the Criminally Insane. She told him he would be eligible for parole after ten years, knowing in her heart that he would never be granted parole. She also convinced him that his chances of survival were better there than in the general population at the Trenton State Prison, where the beating and raping of child molesters was considered an indoor sport.

Stanford went with Detective Pinto to see the Gomez parents. They had achieved somewhat of an empathetic relationship with them after the initial problems between them and Detective Shack.

Maria Gomez answered the door, looking pale and broken. She informed them that she and Elizer had broken up shortly after the murders. She had blamed him for being too strict with them, and he had blamed her for bringing them to America in the first place. He had returned to the Dominican Republic, having no interest in the American justice system and its penalties. He had suffered the greatest penalty—the loss of his two children. He vowed never to return to this "godless country, America."

She was still working at the factory. She wanted to go back to the Dominican Republic as well, but she couldn't leave her two angels, who were buried at Holy Cross Cemetery in North Arlington. She visited them every weekend, more if she could get a ride. She thought Perez should be executed, but she would go along with a deal as long as he never got out of jail. She didn't have much interest in the proceedings and told them that she could not appear at any hearings or sentencing. Stanford made a mental note to have his friend, the school psychologist, see her, as he felt she didn't have much interest in living anymore.

The legal proceedings were signed and notarized by a state Supreme Court judge, and the sentence was pronounced.

Perez made no comment and showed no remorse.

No members of the Gomez family were present. Press coverage was minimal. Yesterday's news.

Perez was incarcerated at Mountain View, Stanford went back to work at school, and life went on.

But nothing was ever the same.

Present Day

CHAPTER 17

The predator, William Albert Perez, had just finished his 3:30 set of exercises. His routine was a hundred push-ups, followed by a hundred sit-ups. He did these five times a day, coordinating his exercise with Mohammed's (his next-door cellmate) prayer times.

A devout Muslim, Mohammed faced Mecca and prayed five times a day at the prescribed times. Once before sunrise, again at one thirty and three thirty in the afternoon, then seven thirty, and finally after sundown anytime between eight and midnight.

Perez liked Mohammed. He didn't like many people. He was very smart and religious. He taught him that Mohammed was the most common first name in the world. He also told him how he wound up here.

A hardworking, legal immigrant from Palestine, he owned a small convenience store in Paterson. His teenage daughter, Fatwa, was rebellious and wouldn't wear the required head-covering *hijab*. She also started having sex with an older man. An older, married black man. He demanded she stop. She wouldn't.

He then did what any righteous Muslim man would do. He took the dagger he had sneaked into the United States from Palestine twenty-five years ago and stabbed the man and the man's wife and child to death.

While being held without bail for trial, his wife, Fatima, visited him and informed him that their daughter had killed herself. Fatima was returning to Palestine, and she would never see him again.

Perez decided that he would not fuck with this dude. Perez's exercise routine, along with the tasteless institutional food, had transformed him from a chubby Puerto Rican doughboy into a sleek, sinewy machine, thirty pounds lighter than when he arrived.

He had the barber shave his head regularly, as he didn't have much hair left anyway, and let his beard grow long. This gave him the appearance of a beige, muscular Amish farmer.

A guard he didn't know told him to go to the staff cafeteria to clean up after a party. He made a few dollars as a trustee, doing menial chores like this. Upon entering, he saw a group of men leaving, luncheon garbage strewn behind them. They were shaking hands and waving Lamont Johnson goodbye and good luck. Apparently, the black fuck was retiring.

He hated Johnson. Shortly after he first arrived at Mountain View Hospital for the Criminally Insane, Johnson and some other guards had given him a bad beating. For nothing. All because of that faggot, Willy Perez. Willy had been flirting with him in the shower, saying that maybe they were cousins or something while leering at his cock with his gay smile. When the predator started smacking him around and trying to buttfuck him, the queer started screaming and yelling, which got him in big trouble.

"The *maricon* wanted it. Why did he start yelling?" the predator reasoned to himself. He made him pay for that many times over the next thirty years.

While Johnson was packing up his retirement gifts, the predator noticed that he was much thinner and unsteady on his feet. One of the guards, who he also didn't know, hugged him and said, "Watch that sugar, man." Apparently, he was sick in some way. Good, thought the predator. I hope he dies soon.

In truth, Johnson suffered from diabetes and was forced to take a medical retirement. The staff was being reduced drastically. That's why Perez didn't recognize any of these guards; they were transferred in from other mental hospitals that had already closed down.

As he swept up under a table, he noticed a gift card envelope that had been dropped on the floor. He surreptitiously slipped it in his pocket, thinking maybe there was money in it. He would check it out later in private.

After he finished cleaning up, he returned to his cell for the evening headcount. He tore open the envelope and saw not cash but a gift subscription to Sports Illustrated magazine.

He hated sports but liked the Sports Illustrated swimsuit edition. He had stolen it out of the hallway one year and used it to jerk off. The models were a little old for his taste, but any port in a storm.

Before he threw it out, he noticed the envelope had Johnson's home address on it: 100 High Street, Apartment 301, Newark, New Jersey.

He tucked that away for safekeeping. He would like to visit Johnson someday to wish him a happy retirement.

Sterling Hardaway strutted around his large corner office in Mountain View Hospital in his usual attire: a crisp white shirt, a red tie, and a gray suit jacket, trying to project an image of a hardworking everyman. He was anything but that.

The Ivy League grad was appointed by his former fraternity brother, the governor of New Jersey, to be the superintendent of the state hospital system. He was, in reality, an effete hatchet man, doing the governor's dirty work by downsizing the expensive budget item of mental health care.

His appearance reminded people of William Daniels, the actor who played a prissy medical administrator in the old TV drama *St. Elsewhere*. He encouraged and enjoyed that comparison.

By following his plan to close old, expensive-to-operate mental hospitals and replace them with halfway houses and outright discharges, he was able to trim millions from the state budget, a campaign promise of his pal, the governor.

Of course, sending these patients back into society loaded up on Prozac and other medications did not work. They soon stopped taking their medications and wound up homeless on city streets or in overcrowded jails.

Hardaway also slashed hundreds of jobs, sending these workers to the swelling unemployment line. The rank-and-file workers hated him, referring to him as "Hardaway, the hardon."

When he first arrived at Mountain View, he ordered the parole board to review all patients who had been denied release in the past few years. The parole board members were all appointed by his pal, the governor, and were eager to rubber-stamp his decisions.

He then had his shapely secretary, Shawanda, compile a list of these miscreants. He had brought her along with him from a hospital in Newark that he had recently gutted. She was dumb as a brick, but she was loyal and had a great rack.

He was working his way through the list, releasing and reassigning dangerous people into society. "Shawanda, have Willy Perez brought up here as soon as possible. This poor man has been in here for too long. He has a sister in Jersey City who's willing to take him in. With the proper medication and an ankle monitor, he should be fine," he concluded pompously.

Shawanda dutifully fired up her computer and scrolled down an alphabetical list of patients, coming to:

PEREZ, William Albert 600167

She notified the guard on-duty in the superintendent's office to bring him up immediately. Had she scrolled one more name down, she would have seen:

PEREZ, Willy Balthazar 600168

He was the correct person. But she didn't. The guard, who was new, did as he was told and brought William Albert Perez to the superintendent's office. The predator had no idea why he was being walked up there, but he went along quietly.

Inside the swanky office, Hardaway greeted him with his cheesy smile and a "Hello, Willy, congratulations."

The predator had no idea what the fuck he was talking about and responded with a blank stare.

"You don't look happy, Willy. You're going home to your sister's house," the superintendent went on. "Of course, there will be conditions, an ankle monitor, and continued use of your medications with regular visits from your parole officer."

The predator thought to himself, *I don't have a sister*. But he played along, saying, "Oh yes, that'll be great."

"Let's see now," Hardaway said as he looked at the report. "Your sister, Sol Pellot, lives at 21 Sip Avenue, in Jersey City."

"That's right," Perez answered, now starting to figure out what was going on. *This moron thinks I'm Willy Perez and is letting me out*, he thought to himself, barely able to control himself.

"We'll notify her to pick you up tomorrow at 9:00 a.m. sharp," Hardaway gushed. "The parole officer will come to the house soon to check things out and fit you with the anklet. Stay in the house until he comes. They're very busy. It might take a few days," he pronounced.

"Oh yessir, Mr. Superintendent. I'll do that, but could you do me a favor?" Perez said, oozing insincerity. "My sister's been so good to me all these years. I'd like to surprise her tomorrow at the house. Please don't call her."

"Absolutely, a capital idea. It will be a fine surprise," Hardaway replied with equal insincerity.

CHAPTER 19

The predator's mind was racing as he returned to his cell. This was too good to be true, but he had to plan how to play it.

He wouldn't say anything to anybody, including his friend Mohammed. He had to keep this quiet so they wouldn't discover their mistake.

He didn't sleep a wink that night, planning and scheming his next move. All he could think of was that he had to get out of this place.

When Mohammed finished his predawn prayers and left for breakfast in the cafeteria, Perez slipped into his cell. He knew Mohammed had cash hidden in his Koran. He had told him that when he was first sent here, his brother sold the convenience store, stole most of the money, and sneaked a little at him during a visit. Perez needed more money than the meager two hundred he had saved up doing trustee work for forty years. He helped himself to Mohammed's hidden stash. There were almost a thousand bucks in the Benjamins and twenties. "Perfect," he rejoiced.

A guard picked him up and walked him down to the intake area, handed him a bag with his old clothes, and told him to change into them and leave the orange jumpsuit behind in the dressing room. As he put on the wrinkled suit his defense attorney had brought him to wear to his court appearances, he found it to be too big as he had lost so much weight. He tightened the belt to his last hole, making it as tight as possible, realizing this was the first time he had worn a belt in forty years. There were no belts in jail.

The next thing he knew, he was walking out of the entrance to the street. A car pulled up to the entrance, and a good-looking nurse got out.

The driver yelled to him, "Uber! Uber!"

He yelled back, confused, "Willy!"

The driver said, "I'm your Uber driver. Dr. Wiley, get in." The predator felt he had to get out of there as fast as possible, fearing someone would take him back to jail. He jumped in the open door of the back seat that the driver was gesturing to. He vaguely remembered learning about this Uber thing on TV—that they were like a cab service.

The driver said, "Hi, Doc. I'm Larry. I'll take you to the hospital now. I had to drop the nurse off here, so dispatch thought I'd kill two birds with one stone."

"Yes, two birds were killed," the predator mumbled.

Larry kept up an annoying stream of conversation as they drove through local streets. After a few miles, the street signs said they were entering Newark.

"So how long have you been at the Special Surgery Hospital, Doc?" Larry asked.

"Oh, quite a while," the predator bluffed back. "As a matter of fact, I'm in a hurry now, Larry. I've got a couple of people who need my special surgery really badly."

They pulled up to the entrance of Newark Beth Israel Hospital, which contained a section for special surgery.

Larry said, "I'll put the fare on the hospital account. Would you like to add a gratuity?" figuring he might get a good tip from a doctor in a hurry.

The predator removed a crisp twenty from his pocket and gave it to Larry.

"Wow, thanks, Doc. Next time you need a ride, ask for me. Larry, Larry Byrd, like the basketball player but with a 'y.'"

Perez didn't know any Larry Bird. *Why was this guy always talking about birds?* He wondered to himself. He exited the Uber and started walking into the first entrance. He didn't know if the bird guy was watching him, so he tried to look like he belonged.

Since he left prison, he had had an overwhelming feeling that people were watching him. It was a natural feeling, being that people had been watching him for a long time, every day and every night.

He decided he would not go back. If they caught up to him, he would die before going back. And some other people were gonna die, too.

CHAPTER 20

The predator waited in the hospital lobby for a few minutes to make sure the damn Uber guy wasn't killing two more birds. While passing time, he asked at the information desk about directions to 100 High Street in Newark. It turned out that he wasn't far away—within walking distance, actually.

"I think I'll pay my old friend Lamont a visit," he said out loud. He saw people look at him strangely and realized that he had to stop this habit of talking to himself out loud, which he had done all the time in prison. He also had to get some different clothes and shave off his long beard. It made him too easy to identify.

While walking in the direction of High Street, the South Ward neighborhood was getting rougher and darker in complexion. He knew he didn't fit in here and had to get to Hudson County, where his fellow *Boricuas* were predominant.

He stopped at a Baptist church, rang the bell, and asked for a handout. The black pastor scowled at him and told him to go two blocks further down to the Salvation Army mission. "They could help you with clothes," he grunted as he slammed the door with force.

"Yeah, I'm in the wrong neighborhood," he said to himself, "but not for long."

The good sisters in the Salvation Army were kind to him, and he left wearing jeans, a gray sweatshirt, and a baseball cap. He threw out the suit.

His stomach was rumbling. He hadn't really eaten in a day and a half. He stopped at a CVS, went in, and bought a three-pack of disposable razors and a small can of aerosol shaving cream, paying in cash. In the CVS men's room, he shaved his long beard, leaving hair all over the sink.

"I really need to eat something," he said aloud, forgetting not to talk to himself again. He spotted a cozy luncheonette, "Pops," which looked decent. Lunchtime was ending, and the place was emptying out. An older black man leaving held the door for him, calling out over his shoulder, "I'll see you for dinner, Pops. What's the special again?"

"Fried fish on Friday, you know that, Lamont," the counterman answered.

"Shit!" the predator exclaimed, pulling his baseball cap down over his eyes and turning his head away. *What luck*, he thought. Here was his prey, right in front of him. He backed away, making believe he dropped something on the sidewalk, then dove into a doorway.

His eyes followed Lamont Johnson as he walked the half block to 100 High Street, an old, WWII-era apartment house. A plan started to form in his poisoned mind.

Now he was really hungry. He went into "Pops" and ordered the lunch special, devouring it greedily. He said to Pops, "You know, I thought I saw an old friend of mine leaving here before, Lamont Johnson. Do you know him?"

Pops grunted. "No."

"Yeah, I used to work with him at the prison," the predator added.

Pops started wiping down the counter at the other end, thinking, *My black ass, you worked with him. You're an ex-con. I have to tell Lamont that at dinner tonight, some PR was looking for him.*

"Never heard of him," he said aloud to the predator. "You want dessert?"

Lamont Johnson took the self-serve elevator—that was always breaking down—up to his third-floor apartment, put on an old vinyl album, and relaxed in his recliner. He favored the old Motown groups—The Temps, The Four Tops, and Marvin. He didn't go this hip-hop shit; he would tell the young guys at Pops. He drifted off to sleep as Ray Charles was singing, "He had Georgia on his mind."

As he was snoring softly, the predator was walking around the building, casing the joint. Lamont awoke at 4 o'clock and went to the bathroom to freshen up for dinner. He was licking his chops, anticipating the fried fish "Pops" made.

The predator, who had been waiting outside his door, listening to his preparation, dashed down the hall and called the elevator to the third floor. He got inside and held down the "Door Close" button.

Johnson approached the elevator and pressed the "Down" button, but it didn't open. After a while, it started beeping, indicating some sort of problem.

"Damn," he said. "Damn, elevator's always breaking here." He gave up and started walking toward the long flight of metal-tipped, linoleum-covered stairs. He was almost there when he thought he heard the elevator doors open behind him.

The predator sprinted out of the elevator and caught Johnson at the top of the stairs, turning toward him. He placed both hands firmly on his chest and pushed as hard as he could, sending the older man crashing down the stairs backward.

Johnson landed at the foot of the stairs, limbs askew, looking like a broken marionette. His skull was fractured, and his neck was broken. Quite dead.

"Happy retirement, boss," the predator bade him farewell, entering the waiting elevator and leaving into the night.

After killing Lamont Johnson, William Albert Perez worked his way back by bus to Hudson County. He had to get a new name, an ID, and some wheels. He used to be able to hotwire a car pretty easily, but now the cars were all different. He wasn't sure if he could still do it.

There was a bar back in the day in West New York where you could get those things, but he doubted it was still there after all these years. He found it eventually, and the sign out front still said "JUNIORS."

He went in. A skinny guy in his forties said, "Hi, *papi*." He responded with an icy glare and flashed the Latin Kings gang sign.

The guy laughed at him. "Oh, *papi*, we don't do that anymore." Perez didn't like this asshole dissing him with his *papi* shit. Inside, he would have snapped his scrawny neck, but right now, he might need him.

"I was friends with Junior Alvarado, who ran this place," Perez said menacingly.

"Yes, he was my father. He died two years ago," Alvarado answered with more respect now, seeing this was a serious man. "I'm Junior Alvarado Jr. They call me Junior-Junior. What can I help you with?" he asked, extending his hand.

"I need an ID, a car, and some help to locate some old friends," Perez stated firmly.

"You got cash? I can help you. We're a full-service establishment," Junior-Junior said cockily. "We rent cars by the day or hour. Do you have a license?" he asked.

"No," Perez said.

"We can help you with that. Who do you want to locate?"

Perez handed him a scrap of paper with the names on it.

"J-3, come here." Junior-Junior beckoned a young guy who looked like a college student over to the bar. "This is my son, Junior Alvarado III, J-3," he said proudly.

"Good," Perez responded. "How much?"

"A thousand for a valid NJ driver's license, fifty an hour for a car, and twenty-five per person research fees. Payable in cash up front, now," Junior-Junior concluded.

Perez took out most of the cash he had stolen from Mohammed and gave it to him. Junior-Junior counted it out as skillfully as any bank teller, saying, "You're a little short, but I'll give you a discount, being that you ran with my father." He took out a business card that read simply: *JUNIOR-JUNIOR.* "Take this to the motor vehicle office in North Bergen. Fill out some papers and get in line for Oswaldo Jimenez. He's the only Spanish guy there. You can't miss him. All the other clerks are fat White women. When you give him the forms, put my card on top. He'll tell you what to do."

"But what form do I fill out?" asked Perez.

"Doesn't matter. Just hand him something. Make it look good," Junior-Junior said dismissively. "Now go with J-3. He'll get your information."

They sat down at a small table off the side of the bar, where J-3 had several laptops set up. He took the three names and started typing furiously. After only a few minutes, he handed Perez a printout that read:

1.　*Gladys Orozco—deceased, 2008.*

Good, Perez thought. That was his second cousin who hit him with the frying pan when her ten-year-old daughter tried to seduce him. He wondered why she had stopped coming to his parole hearings, always carrying on about how bad he was.

2.　*Betty Collins—famous psychic, 92 years old. Lives at 200 Orient Way, Rutherford, NJ.*

> 3. *William Stanford—retired educator. Lives at 580 Mountain Road, West Hoboken, NJ.*

"Copy it down on a piece of paper and give me the printout back," J-3 said cautiously. It amazed Perez that all that information could be found so fast with these computers. It was a good thing he hadn't smacked Junior-Junior, he thought.

As he was leaving, Junior-Junior told him, "Take the bus to the motor vehicle office. We wouldn't want you driving without a license. That's against the law. When you get the license, come back. I'll rent you a car, so you can go see your friends," he winked with a sinister grin.

Perez followed Junior-Junior's instructions and saw Oswaldo Jimenez at the North Bergen Motor Vehicle Agency. He left an hour later with a valid New Jersey driver's license with his picture on it in the name of Christian Miller. He caught a few hours of sleep in nearby Braddock County Park on a bench.

He returned the next day to Junior's to rent a car.

"Do you have a valid NJ driver's license, sir?" Junior-Junior asked him, like he had never seen him before.

"Yes, I—" Perez started to pull it out to show Junior-Junior, but he grabbed his arm, stopping him, not wanting to see it.

"The insurance card and registration are in the glove compartment. Happy motoring, sir. You have several hours' credit."

What Perez didn't know was that Junior-Junior, Jimenez, and many others were part of a large criminal enterprise with clerks in key positions in several state and county offices. Agents in the Motor Vehicles Dept., Hudson County Clerks offices, the Bureau of Vital Statistics, and other offices all worked together to resurrect infants who had died shortly after birth and provide their clean identities to criminals and illegal aliens. All at a large profit for the key players.

Perez, now Christian Miller, drove out to the Rutherford address that J-3 had sold him for the psychic, Betty Collins. He parked across the street in a quiet residential neighborhood. He wouldn't be able to stay there long, he thought. Too many old White people were walking their dogs.

But suddenly, a pretty but slightly beat-up-looking woman came out of the front door, yelling behind her, "I'm going to ACME, Mom. I'll be back in an hour," she said, pulling the door closed behind her.

An hour—perfect, now Miller thought. *No deadbolt.* He waited until she pulled away in an old Toyota and approached the house. He looked into the front window and saw an old woman in a hospital bed in what was previously a first-floor dining room.

Perez took out his new Christian Miller driver's license and quickly loaded the door, using the plastic card to push back the locking mechanism. He quietly stepped inside, the only sound being the periodic hissing of the oxygen being pumped into her nostrils.

She was dozing, but not for long. In one quick movement, he yanked the oxygen out of her nose while taking one of her pillows from behind her head, forcing it down over her face.

The ill, ninety-two-year-old woman startled awake but had no strength to fight off her attacker. It was over fast.

Perez gently replaced the pillow behind her head, smoothed the covers, put the oxygen tubes back in her nose, and started to leave. He stopped and turned back, placing his index finger and thumb in the corners of her mouth and pushing her lips into a macabre smile.

"Did you see that coming, psychic Betty?" he laughed and left.

Two down, one to go.

Detective Tommy Kelley of the Hudson County Probation Department sat at his desk in the Administration Building in Jersey City.

He was undecided on what to do. He had handicapped the entire race card at Aqueduct and liked several horses. He had a pretty good streak going at the beginning of the winter meet, but then, as always, he cooled off and bet too much trying to get even.

Kelley knew gambling was the worst of his vices, followed closely by drinking and whoring around. Sometimes, he combined all three at once for a trifecta of degeneracy. This code of conduct had resulted in two ex-wives and two large, outstanding credit union loans.

He really should go over to Sip St. and check on this hump, Perez, he thought. He was supposed to set him up with an ankle monitor two weeks ago, but he was so hot at the track that he didn't go. He decided to do it today, then catch the PATH train to Aqueduct. He could still make the late double.

Sol Pellot cracked open her front door in response to the knocking White guy. He wore a jacket and tie, and, in this neighborhood, that meant some kind of law enforcement.

"Sol Pellot," he stated.

"Yes," she answered. "Who are you?"

"Detective Kelly, Hudson County Probation Department," he responded, obliging her.

"Yes?" she answered again.

"I'm here to see your brother, Willy Perez," he stated, growing impatient with the slow pace of the conversation.

"He ain't here," she said, pissed off.

"He's supposed to be here," Kelley responded, now getting fired up. "He was not supposed to leave the house until I got here," he added.

"He didn't leave the house," she replied defensively, her hands on her hips.

"Well then, where the hell is he?" raising his voice.

"He's in jail, you dickhead!" she yelled back.

He opened his briefcase to check the paperwork. His marked-up daily racing form fell out as he frantically shifted papers. "It says here that he was paroled ten days ago and was to report here and await me."

"No, he wasn't. He called me yesterday from jail. He's still there," she said with an icy tone.

Shit, thought Kelley. Some kind of screwup.

"Listen, Ms. Pellot. I'm going to check this out at the jail. There's been some kind of mistake," Kelley stammered.

"Yeah, you better check it out. You guys don't know what the fuck you're doing," she said while closing the door in his face.

This was bad. Kelley thought back to the time a couple years ago when, while riding the train to Aqueduct, he saw a murderer whose wanted poster he had just seen as he left the office. He alerted the conductor surreptitiously, and two Port Authority detectives arrested the perp as they disembarked on the platform. He couldn't have taken credit because he wasn't supposed to even be on the train. He would have gotten a commendation at the very least, maybe a medal.

Later, the PA detectives, trying to be nice, sent a letter praising his alertness to his commander, and he got a seven-day rip.

Kelley sped back to the headquarters, hoping to find out what went wrong. Of course, the fact that it took him two weeks to get his fat Irish ass over there was going to be a problem. He couldn't afford another suspension without pay, given all his debts.

No, he wasn't going to make the late double today, after all.

CHAPTER 24

After killing Betty Collins in Rutherford, Perez calmly drove to the nearby Meadowlands Racetrack. He needed a job and a place to stay. He had experience as a hot walker and groom when he was working at El Comandante Racetrack in San Juan and, before he went to jail, at Penn National Racetrack in western Pennsylvania. This could solve both his needs, as grooms were provided a dormitory bed on the backside.

Using his new ID, he talked his way through the security gate, saying he had a job interview at the Johnny Lutessa barn. Lutessa had a large barn of thirty horses and was always looking for help, as these grooms are transient and unreliable. He demonstrated his skill set with horses to an assistant trainer, and he was hired and given a dorm bed and cafeteria pass.

He had to return the car to Junior-Junior and take a bus back to the track, but first he had one more stop to make in West Hoboken.

He drove to the address of William Stanford. It was a luxury high-rise twenty-two stories tall with a circular driveway in front, surrounding a fountain with multicolored lights. There was only one entrance, and that was staffed by a concierge at a front desk with plenty of cameras.

He had gotten lucky with Lamont Johnson and Betty Collins. However, this wasn't going to be easy. He had to think and make a plan. Stanford might not even be here, as J-3 had said he had an address in Florida, too, but he really wanted to hurt this prick. He would always show up at his parole hearings and tell the story of how he found the bodies of those kids—"Boohoo." The parole board would listen to him intently, with some actually weeping, and deny him quickly.

Oh, he was gonna get his.

At this very moment, Bill Stanford was sitting at the bar in St. Michael's Catholic Men's Club in West Hoboken with his old friend, Tommy Brophy. "Broph" had been taunting him to come in for a beer. They had grown up together, as Stanford lived around the corner from the club. In those days, they had two bowling alleys in which he would occasionally work as a pinboy. It was hard work for low pay, with an occasional pin whacking his shin as he sat on a bench between the two lanes. But he was fifteen and had a lot of energy then, not like now.

Stanford's back ached as he remembered why he didn't like to drink there—the bar stool had no backrest. He had arthritis in his back, and the cold in New Jersey made it worse. He asked himself, *What was he even doing here at this time of year?* He should've left for Florida two weeks ago. But he hated the long drive down by himself, and something was just telling him not to go yet.

As he was cursing the pinboy job for screwing up his back, Georgie Summers, the three-hundred-pound bartender, started yelling at him and pointing to the ancient color TV mounted at the end of the bar. It wasn't a flat screen; it was a fat screen with tubes.

News 12 New Jersey was on, and a pretty girl who was probably trying to get a job on a real New York station was reporting a story with her "solemn girl" act.

Summers was saying, "Duke, Duke, it's that guy they're talking about." Summers was using his high school nickname, which only about five living people still called him.

As he started to hear what the reporter was saying, it became apparent that William Albert Perez was released from prison for some kind of mistake.

Summers was one of the few people who remembered that he was involved in the case. He quickly excused himself to hear this completely at home as News 12 New Jersey repeated their stories, like, every hour.

At home, catching the story from the beginning an hour later, it seemed that Perez was let go by mistake. The governor was approving a special investigation to find out how this happened. A clerk,

Shawanda Jones, and a Hudson County parole officer, Thomas Kelley, had already been terminated, and the governor's frat brother, Sterling Hardaway, had been reassigned to the Department of Fish and Game.

Maybe I'll put off the trip back to Florida a little longer, Stanford thought.

That night, Stanford couldn't sleep. He kept ruminating about what he should do. At about 3:30 in the morning, he decided that he would definitely stay in New Jersey and find Perez. He chewed a few of his THC edible gummies and finally got to sleep.

The next morning, he wrote down his plan on a piece of paper, listing pros and cons on either side. He used to do this in college to help organize his thoughts.

The negatives were: (a) he was old and twenty pounds over his playing weight with a bad back; (b) he had no legal standing any-more; and (c) his political connections had died or gone to prison. On the positive side, however, he was very familiar with the area, the case itself, and that sicko Perez.

He listed the stops he would make today in order—visit the prison; visit Betty Collins, the psychic; and talk to his Hispanic underworld connections in West Hoboken to see if anyone heard anything about Perez's whereabouts. After spending thirty-two years in the local school system and political scene, he knew a lot of people in town, good and bad.

He drove out to Newark and entered the lobby of Mountain View Mental Hospital for the Criminally Insane. He didn't get far. There was maximum security in effect as they were trying to recover from the embarrassing faux pas of releasing the wrong Perez—a little like closing the barn door after the horse ran away.

He tried unsuccessfully to talk to security to explain his interest in the case and who he was. They didn't care. They blew him off and asked him firmly to leave. To them, he was just some old guy with a white beard and ponytail who was interfering with their important work. He felt like Cagney in that old movie where he got gunned down on the steps of the church and the cop leans over his body and says, "Yeah, he used to be somebody."

Discouraged and battling his growing anxiety, he started to leave when an older guard stopped him.

"I remember you, dude. You used to come down to the parole hearings for that squirrel. Lamont Johnson said that you were good people."

"Oh, thanks," Stanford replied, seizing a glimmer of hope. "Is Johnson around? I'd like to talk to him."

"I would too, but Lamont passed away recently, not long after he retired. It happens to us guys a lot. That's why I want to retire."

"Shit, I'm sorry, man." Stanford pushed on. "Does he have any friends or family I could speak to?"

"He hung out at Pops in the South Ward, down the block from where he lived. Everyone knew him there." As he said that, he put his hand in the small of Stanford's back, gently guiding him out the door. "You got to leave now," he whispered. "I'm getting the stink eye from the boss for talking to you."

He understood and left. He got in his car and drove to Rutherford. It wasn't far, but the streets looked different from the last time he had been there. He drove around for a while until he found Betty Collins's house on Orient Way. It looked a little run-down.

He parked out front and rang the bell. A pretty, sixty-something-looking woman answered the door, facing him with a blank stare. "Yes?" she asked. Like the house, she looked a little run-down.

"I'm Bill Stanford. I'm an old friend of Betty Collins. Does she still live here?"

"No, she doesn't live here or anywhere else. She died recently," she said with a mix of attitude and sorrow.

"Oh, I'm sorry. I didn't know. I don't really watch the news anymore."

"It wasn't on the news. She hasn't been famous for twenty years. They don't care anymore." More attitude.

"I worked with her on a case involving missing children many years ago. I thought she could help me," Stanford said, trying his formerly boyish grin.

She stared at him for what seemed like ages, then smiled. "Yeah, I remember you. She liked you. Come in," Carol said.

Stanford explained the release of Perez and his efforts to return him to jail. She smiled again, softly saying, "Aren't you a little old for this shit?"

He realized that he looked a little run-down, too. His appearance fit more down in Florida but not so much up here. Properly said, he looked like an overweight Willie Nelson.

"I remember when you brought that box of letters out to my mother. I thought you were very kind. You didn't treat my mother like a freak."

Stanford had forgotten but now remembered that after his picture with Betty appeared in a national tabloid newspaper, he received a hundred letters from parents and relatives looking for their missing children. Desperate, they sent letters with pieces of clothing, money, or anything else if he and Betty would find their child. He returned the money and told them by letter that he would give all the information to Betty, and maybe she could help them. He wasn't a detective, but he would pray for their safe return.

"Did your mom ever help any of those people?" he asked Carol as she poured them both a glass of red wine. Stanford liked red wine. Dr. Oz said on TV that two glasses of red wine a day were good for your health, so he figured that six or seven a day would be really good for his health. She laughed at his jokes. She liked red wine, too.

"Yes, she located a few of the children, some dead but a few alive."

"How did she die, Carol?"

"Oh, she had heart problems and respiratory issues. Everything was failing. She spent the last year or so in a hospital bed down here. I had to do everything for her. Why do you ask?"

"It's just that this Perez gets out of jail, and then two people involved in the case die right around the same time: your mom and a prison guard named Johnson."

"Well, she died of natural causes. I went to the store for a few minutes, and she died before I got back." Carol was wringing her hands as she spoke, and he noticed that they were red and raw.

She saw him looking at them and shrugged. "I kept everything very clean. I scrubbed everything. She was prone to lung infections. I did my best." Her voice broke as she wiped a tear away.

"So nothing was disturbed or anything?" he asked.

"No, she was just asleep, very peaceful-looking. The police came, but there was no investigation. She was ninety-two and had all kinds of problems. What happened to Johnson?" she asked.

"I'm not sure how he died, but I'm going out tomorrow to find out. Want to join me?" She smiled and said yes.

He remembered that she had been a knockout when she was younger. He had hit on her, even though he was married. She said she had a boyfriend and brushed him off then. "Do you still have that boyfriend?" he asked.

"No. Do you still have that wife?"

"No," he smiled. "It's a date. I'll pick you up at 2:00."

Stanford was nervous as he prepared for his date with Carol. He hadn't been on a real date in some time. She was pretty, and she seemed to like him. He didn't want to screw this up. He wore his go-to black jeans and one of his less worn-out T-shirts. He popped half a Klonopin that his doctor had prescribed for anxiety and went to pick her up.

Carol was nervous as she prepared for her date with Bill frantically. She hadn't been on a real date for some time while caring for her mother. She liked him. He was funny and not bad-looking. She thought about taking a tranquilizer but resisted, not wanting to go down that road again. She fixed her hair and makeup as best as she could and was ready on time when he picked her up.

He opened the car door for her, which she liked. "Where are we going?" she asked as they pulled away.

"Well, we're going to a highly recommended restaurant in Newark," he smiled confidently.

"Newark?" she asked, never knowing when this guy was serious and joking.

"Yes, I want to talk to some people there about Lamont Johnson. It might help me find Perez. This prick's dangerous, and I want to find him."

"You know, Bill. I was thinking last night after you left about my mother's death, and there was one strange thing I had forgotten."

Stanford turned sharply toward her, taking his eyes off the road momentarily. "Really, what?"

"I was always careful about keeping her and the place clean."

Stanford's mind flashed back to the night of her chapped hands. "Yeah, I could see that, Carol."

"Well, that day when I came back, I thought I smelled an odor."

"What kind of odor?" Stanford queried.

"It kind of had a funky, sour smell like BO, but I was so upset that it didn't really register."

"Hmm," Stanford grunted as they neared Newark and were proceeding through some sketchy neighborhoods. He could see out of the corner of his eye that she was looking around unhappily. He found a parking space down the block from Pops. She looked like she didn't want to get out of the car.

"Well, I hope you're hungry. The food is supposed to be great here," said Bill, pulling her out of the seat.

They entered Pops, which wasn't too crowded. He purposely picked this time, around 2:30, for that reason. An old-fashioned jukebox was cranking out some old Motown hits. They sat at the counter. They were the only white faces in the room. An older black man behind the counter approached them.

"Hi, you, Pops?" Stanford asked.

"Yeah, you lost?" Pops replied.

"Ah, we'd like to eat here." Pops just stared at them.

"I'd also like to ask you about Lamont Johnson. I'm told he was a friend of yours."

"You're too old to be a cop," Pops said, then turned to Carol, "and you're too pretty."

"No, I'm not a cop, but I'm interested in finding that guy who got out of the jail Lamont worked at."

Pops's mood softened, and he said, "Lamont came in here every day. He'd eat and listen to the old songs."

"How did he die?" Stanford asked.

"They said he fell down his stairs, but that's bullshit."

"Why do you say that? Did the cops investigate?" Stanford asked.

"Cops didn't do shit. A sick old Black man fell down the stairs. No concern of theirs. And I told them about that guy, too, but they paid me no mind."

"What guy, Pops?"

"The guy who was in here that very day asked about him, saying he worked with him. But he was a con. I know it," Pops spit out.

"What did he look like? This guy?"

"Spanish, not young, well-built." Pops looked up, trying to remember.

Stanford pulled his cell phone out and showed a picture of Perez. "Was it this guy?"

"Could be. He didn't have a beard, though. Could be," Pops said, looking again at the picture.

Carol hadn't appeared too interested in the conversation—she just wanted to get out of there—but she now started to pay attention. This goofy guy, Stanford, might be smarter than he looks.

"You two want to eat now? I'll make you something nice," Pops said, now friendly. He served them two heaping disks of fried fish that they devoured hungrily.

"This is delicious," Carol gushed.

"Yeah, fried fish—Friday specialty on the house—Lamont's favorite. When he didn't come in that Friday, I knew something was wrong," Pops continued. "I wish I had taken a better look at that guy, but I couldn't wait to get him out of here."

"Why is that?" Carol asked.

"Man had the worst BO I ever smelled. Like he was sleeping rough."

Carol and Stanford turned to look at each other at the same time and nodded silently. Stanford paid the check with cash, and they started to leave. Pops said, "You two come back now, any time for a fish fry on Friday. It was nice to meet you, Mr..."

"Moore, Sam Moore," Stanford replied as "Soul Man" blasted away on the jukebox.

"Yeah, right, Mr. Sam Moore, and I suppose she's Diana Ross."

"No, no, Mary Wilson," Stanford answered.

As he drove Carol home, he asked, "Did you like the food?"

"Yes, but what was that bit about Sam Moore?" Carol asked.

"I didn't want to use our real names, and Soul Man was playing, so I said Sam Moore. He's half of the Memphis soul group, Sam & Dave. That was one of their best hits."

"How did you know that?" she asked.

"Oh, I met him once in Atlantic City."

"Really, how?"

"Joe Cocker introduced us backstage." Joe Cocker she had heard of.

"How'd that happen?" she asked.

"I'll tell you on our next date," he grinned.

"And Mary Wilson, you met her too, I suppose," she said.

"Yes, I did—in Atlantic City. No, Barbados. She was the pretty Supreme and was doing a one-woman show based on the life of Lena Home. We had a nice chat."

Carol didn't know if this guy had a really interesting life or had a great line of shit, but she decided she would like to find out.

"Next Friday? Dinner at Pops?" she asked.

"My treat," he answered. *Great, I've met the girl of my dreams*, he thought.

A day or two passed, and Stanford couldn't stop thinking about Carol. He couldn't wait for next Friday to see her again. He called her up.

"Hi, Bill," Carol answered, "what have you been up to?"

"I'm trying to figure out where this Perez guy might be. I'm sure he had something to do with your mother's death and Lamont Johnson's."

"Why don't you just let the police handle it and go back to Florida?" she said it kind of sharply. He was a little taken aback by her tone.

"I think he might be around this area," Stanford went on. "You know, like, in his comfort zone."

There was a silent, tense pause.

"You're right. He's in this area, and he's very close," she blurted out.

"Have you seen him?" he asked.

"Not with my own eyes, but he's here, and he's a danger to you. Please go to Florida now.

"So you do have your mother's gift," he stated emphatically.

"Yes, I do. I always denied it. The kids at school made fun of me and called Mom a witch. I didn't want to be known as her crazy daughter. I just wanted to be a normal kid. But I see things too."

"Okay, look. Let's go out tonight and discuss this. I know a good place, not far from you—the Park Tavern near the train station. Great food and a nice crowd. We could eat and catch a few races after at the track."

"I know the place. I used to go there with my boyfriend, Peter. He lived in Fort Lee and figured no one would know him there. He was married."

"Oh, I didn't know that." Stanford was honestly surprised.

"Yes, he had a beautiful wife, three kids, and a dog in a million-dollar house in Fort Lee. He also had a big, high-end dental practice up there. He kept promising to leave her, but there was always some excuse—one son was graduating from high school, and the daughter was leaving for music school. He just strung me along. I was a fool, and he used me," she said bitterly.

"I'm sorry he hurt you like that, but you're beautiful. Why did you stay with him? I'm sure there were plenty of guys interested in you," Stanford said, trying to console her.

"I should have, but he also had a big prescription pad that supplied me with unlimited oxy and Percocet. He strung me along and strung me out."

"I'll pick you up at five. We'll go to the Park Tavern if it doesn't bring back too many bad memories. We'll make some new, happy memories. I'll tell you the story of how I smoked a joint with Sam Kenison."

She laughed and groaned. "Oh no, another Atlantic City story."

"No, silly, Vegas baby," he laughed and hung up.

They arrived at the Park Tavern at five and got a booth in the back dining room away from the noisy and nosey people at the bar. Some of his friends, Emil, Rick, and Phil, snuck peeks at him and his beautiful date and gave him the silent thumbs-up sign.

He wanted to talk quietly with her and find out more about her visions. Her mother had told him years ago that it was like a short scene from a movie would just run through her head. She couldn't summon it on command; it just happened randomly without warning. Carol said it was that way with her, too, and she was warned that this monster would hurt him next. That's why she wanted him to go to Florida soon.

He said that he would go if she would come with him. "Look, it's a long ride by myself. I have plenty of room in my condo. Stay a week. If you hate it, you can fly home. I have Sirius XM in my car, and I'll tell you the story of my life for eighteen hours on the road. You'll love it."

He was impressively charming. She said, "I'll think about it."

They had a nice dinner, spaghetti with meat sauce—his favorite—and some red wine, then went to the Meadowlands. He picked up a program and steered her to the walking ring in the paddock. He preferred to handicap a day in advance, using the daily racing form, but this was a spur-of-the-moment trip. He would just check the horses out before the race and make some bets on their appearance. He was pretty good at this, having owned thoroughbreds in the 80s and 90s. His trainer, Johnny Lutessa, had some horses entered. He would try to catch his eye and introduce him to Carol. That might impress her.

As the horses circled the paddock, Johnny Lutessa saw him at the rail, waved, and made a gesture with an envelope he was holding. Stanford immediately understood his sign language: he was going to drop a claim on a horse in this race. The special envelope had to be placed in the claim box no later than ten minutes before the race began. After the race, win or lose, dead or alive, the horse was yours, provided you had enough money in your account to cover the price. Stanford waved back, indicating he understood that Lutessa had a time constraint and would see him later.

While this was happening, Carol's mood changed drastically, from jovial to terrified. She was trembling in a cold sweat.

"What's wrong?" Stanford asked.

She couldn't speak. She just pointed at a gray horse being saddled in front of them. "It's him," she finally choked out. "The groom."

Stanford looked. The groom did look like Perez, but he had a hat down over his eyes. He couldn't be sure.

"Let's get out of here," he said.

Carol grabbed his arm. "Call the police," she begged.

"No. I have a better idea."

Stanford had lied to Carol about recognizing Perez. He was sure it was him but feigned uncertainty to buy himself time.

He thought long and hard and came up with a plan. Perez was never going to be free to kill again. He had to gather up the stuff he would need to end this once and for all.

He dug out his father's .38 police special from its hiding place and checked it out. His father, William G. Stanford, had been a Jersey City policeman like his grandfather, William B. Stanford. Stanford had gone target shooting with Pinto and some other cops at the old Sohuetzen Park firing range and used this weapon. He was a decent shot but was a little out of practice. He would have to be close.

He looked over the advance racing form and saw that Johnny Lutessa had several horses entered on Thursday night's card. Odds were at least one of them would have Perez as a groom, putting him where he could see him.

Stanford then rummaged through his desk for one of his old New Jersey owner's licenses. They were all expired, and in the picture on the front, he was clean-shaven with short hair. He would fix that today with a quick trip up to North Bergen to see Dominick, his barber for forty years. It was amazing that in all the years, Dominick's Italian accent never changed; it was actually heavier now. Stanford hadn't had a haircut in a year and a half and told Dom to trim the beard down to almost nothing and lose the ponytail.

Upon leaving the track last night, he had seen signs advertising a rock concert following the Thursday night races. One of the groups was the Billy Hector Band. He was an old friend of Billy Hector for many years. Perfect.

It would be loud and crowded with young people enjoying the music and the three-dollar beer specials on the track following the races. This event was an attempt to bring a younger demographic to the track to replace the old-timers who were dying out or too infirm to go to the track anymore.

It never worked. The kids came for the show, didn't watch the races, and didn't bet. But it would make for a perfect diversion.

Stanford called Carol on Thursday morning and begged her to join him on Friday afternoon for a farewell fish dinner at Pops, then drive with him down to Pass-A-Grille, Florida.

"I don't know, Bill. It's kind of sudden," Carol replied. "I like you a lot, but…"

"Look, Carol," Stanford interrupted, "you told me I was in danger and to go back to Florida. I'm doing what you want, but I want you with me. I've become fond of you in a short time. Let's go down there and see what happens. Like I said, if you hate it, you can fly back whenever, but we have a lot of fun together," he pleaded.

"We do, Bill," she conceded. "Alright, I'll try it, but on such short notice. I'll need all day today to get packed and ready for Friday afternoon." Carol's voice finally held some enthusiasm.

"You don't need much, Car; some shorts, T-shirts, some bathing suits, and flip-flops. It's very casual down there. You could pack in an hour." Stanford was in full sales mode.

"I'll pick you up at 4:30. We'll get the special at Pops and leave right from there. It's close to the Turnpike, and we'll drive the first night to Fayetteville in North Carolina. There's less traffic than we'll hit in DC at a good time." Stanford's confidence reassured Carol that he obviously had made this trip many times.

Great, Stanford thought; Friday's agenda was set, and he had his action plan for Thursday night. All he needed was a little luck and his gift of bullshit to get him in the right place. *But do I have the balls to do this?* he thought.

Stanford drove to the track in time for the third race. Lutessa had horses entered in the third, fourth, and last races. He parked in the main lot, paid cash for admission and a program, and went in. He saw his reflection in the large glass door and was shocked at his appearance—no beard, short hair, no ponytail. He hadn't looked like this in a while. He had purposely worn old clothes and sneakers he could dispose of after tonight. His fake ID and gun were in the car.

He walked to the padlock to see the horses preparing for the third race. Lutessa's horse was being led by an older Black man. No good.

He repeated this procedure for the fourth race, forty-five minutes later. Again, no good. Lutessa's horse was being walked by a young, tall White guy.

The last race was scheduled to go off at 10:00 p.m., with the rock concert to start immediately after.

Shit, he thought to himself. I didn't check to see if it was scratched. If Lutessa's horse was out of the last race, it would screw up his plan.

He raced over to the scratch board and saw that there were no scratches from the last race. He breathed a deep sigh of relief. *A stupid mistake*, he thought. *I'm not focusing.*

He resisted the strong urge to get a couple of beers while he was waiting for 10 o'clock. No, no more distractions were needed.

Finally, at seventeen minutes to 10:00, the horses were brought in from the barns to the paddock to be paraded and saddled.

Lutessa's horse was being handled by Perez. Perfect.

He stayed back behind some young people, who, as normal, knew nothing about horse racing and had come for the concert.

"Oh, look at the pretty gray one," a young woman with a great rack exclaimed.

"Yeah, beautiful," two young guys responded, looking at her chest and not the horses. At nine minutes to post, the jockeys came around, mounted up, and walked the horses to the post parade on the track.

It was a long race, and Stanford watched to see if anyone claimed the horse. If they claimed Lutessa's horse—the #7 "Got My Grey"—he would have to go back to the test barn after the race. He would also have to be tested if he finished first, second, or third, or if he was unusually bad at the steward's discretion.

Stanford hoped for an out-of-the-money finish as he saw no forms being dropped in the claim box. It was a 1 and 1/16 race for cheap claimers, and Got My Grey's jockey was Joe Bravo, one of the best and honest. He would try his best on the horse. *Good for them, but not for me*, Stanford thought.

The gates sprang open, and the twelve thoroughbreds broke out at full speed. Bravo steered Got My Grey to the rail to save ground as two or three others vied for the head. This was the horses' pattern—lay low, let the frontrunners tire, and close in the stretch.

At the first marker, however, Bravo had the horse closer to the front, a change in tactics. The pace was fast, and Got My Grey was struggling to keep up. As they turned for home, he tired from his earlier exertions and finished an unimpressive sixth.

Stanford quickly headed for the door, pausing to hear the announcement that the race was official; there were no fouls, claims, or inquiries.

As Stanford walked to his car in the parking lot, Perez walked the unsaddled horse back to the barn, where he would be bathed, walked, or cooled out by him. That could take about a half-hour, and it would give the band time to set up and start on the front side.

Stanford went to the parking lot, joined by other patrons who were not staying for the show. He drove his car out of the lot to the stable gate entrance.

This could be a little tricky, he thought to himself as he approached the guard at the gatehouse and rolled down his window.

The bored-looking guard looked up sleepily from his race form, annoyed at the interruption of the night races. Stanford flashed his owner's license, quickly holding his thumb over the expiration date.

He said, "I hope Johnny's got an excuse this time. The horse ran like shit," and he pulled forward. The guard didn't bat an eye, not giving a shit about letting him go into the horse owner's stable.

Stanford parked by the next barn and watched Perez go through his duties methodically with Got My Grey. He put the .38 in the outside pocket of his jacket and wondered why he had been so concerned about getting by the guard. He should have remembered that everybody who worked at the track played horses. That was their major concern, not their job.

Stanford watched as Perez finished his duties with Got My Grey. Shortly thereafter, Perez and another groom left the barn laughing, walking past the manure pile toward the back fence of the stable area.

Stanford followed quietly from a discreet distance. The two found a gap in the fence and went down to Benny's Creek. Stanford wondered what they were up to, as he could hear the music cranking up in the background.

Soon, he got his answer in the pungent, unmistakable odor of pot wafting back toward him. The added groom with Perez created a problem. He did not need a witness or another victim. He decided to sit tight for a while and let them get stoned.

After a while, the other groom told Perez he was going to go listen to the music. Perez replied in Spanish that he was going to stay and have another joint.

"Yes," Stanford whispered. He gave the groom a few minutes to clear the area and quickly squeezed through the fence to the creek.

In one motion, he pulled the revolver out of his jacket and surprised Perez. The stoned killer looked at Stanford groggily, not recognizing him or knowing why he was pointing a gun at him.

"What the fuck?" he slurred as Stanford fired the first shot, hitting him squarely between the eyes. *Pop.*

"That was for Esmi!" Stanford said aloud. He stood over the fallen Perez and fired again into his face. *Pop.* "And that was for Jesus."

Pop. "And Betty Collins."

Pop. "And Lamont Johnson."

Perez's face was now obliterated. His revolver now empty, he carefully wiped it clean with a rag he brought and heaved it as far as he could throw it into Benny's Creek.

He checked Perez's pockets for any ID. Nothing. No money, either. Good. If the body was found, it would take a while to identify him. His body was drifting away as it was high tide, and the current was moving swiftly toward the Hackensack River and eventually Newark Bay.

It occurred to Stanford that Perez might wind up on the shore in Secaucus, near where he brought little Esmi and Jesus. That would be poetic justice.

He was going over all the details in his mind; he didn't want to forget anything. He had wiped off the bullets before he loaded them—wearing gloves—into the revolver.

He had the rag he used to handle Perez and the gun. Returning to his car, he changed into another set of clothes he had brought. He put the jacket, jeans, rag, and sneakers in a plastic bag.

As he started up his car, he heard the Billy Hector Band going into one of their big hits, "You Ain't Nothin' But Fine, Fine, Fine." It was a fine night, indeed.

He drove out of the stable area, passing through the security gate slowly. The guard was still handicapping and never even looked up.

On his way home, he dropped the plastic bag of clothing in a Salvation Army container in Hoboken.

Parking in his allotted slot underneath his high-rise apartment, he glanced full-force at the security camera, smiling. A typical night at the races concluded, should anyone ever check.

EPILOGUE

Sterling Hardaway was arrested and charged with sexual assault of a male game warden in his new position as director of Fish and Game. While in Bergen County Jail, awaiting a bail hearing, he was gang-graped and strangled by several inmates. His friend, the governor, did not attend his funeral. After all, he was up for reelection next year.

Shawanda Jones, the scapegoat in the erroneous release of the killer inmate Perez, became a highly successful exotic dancer in the New York–New Jersey circuit, earning a mid-six-figure yearly income. She was the featured performer at Boomers Gentlemen's Club on the banks of Benny's Creek. Her agent was trying to get her a movie deal.

Under the guise of urban renewal, the landlord of Pops Luncheonette brazenly doubled his rent. Unable to pay, Pops closed the business and retired, dying six months later with all his secrets. The space remains empty to this day.

Stanford and Carol stayed in Florida, enjoying the weather, beaches, and happy hours. She had no desire to return to New Jersey and, after six months, had a real estate agent sell her mother's house in Rutherford. Stanford kept his condo in West Hoboken, just in case.

The body of William Albert Perez, also known as Christian Miller, was never found.

ABOUT THE AUTHOR

William M. Stanton is a native of New Jersey, now living in Pass-a-Grille, Saint Pete Beach, Florida, with the love of his life, Carol.

He is a graduate of Union City. NJ, Emerson High School. He earned a BA degree in education from Montclair State College and an AMA in administration and supervision from Seton Hall University. He retired after thirty-two years of service in the Union City school system as a teacher and administrator.

He also held part-time jobs as director of public information for Riverside General Hospital in Secaucus, New Jersey; assistant to the public safety commissioner in Union City, New Jersey; and bouncer at Meadowbrook Disco in Cedar Grove, NJ.

www.ingramcontent.com/pod-product-compliance
Lightning Source LLC
Chambersburg PA
CBHW022049150726
47990CB00003B/1018